The Helicopters Are Down

The Helicopters Are Down

Indira Parthasarathy

translated from the Tamil by
ANDY SUNDARESAN

hachette
INDIA

First published in Tamil in 1971

This translation first published in 2023 by Hachette India
(Registered name: Hachette Book Publishing India Pvt. Ltd)
An Hachette UK company
www.hachetteindia.com

1

The novel was originally serialized in a literary magazine *Kalki* and later purchased in book form from Tamizh Puthakalayam and the author thanks them for that.

ISBN 978-93-93701-83-1

Hachette Book Publishing India Pvt. Ltd
4th & 5th Floors, Corporate Centre,
Plot No. 94, Sector 44, Gurugram 122003, India

Typeset in Miller Text 11.5/16
by R. Ajith Kumar, New Delhi

Printed and bound in India
by Manipal Technologies Limited

MIX
Paper from responsible sources
FSC™ C043100
FSC www.fsc.org

AUTHOR'S DEDICATION

To my daughter Padma and son-in-law Ram,
who have taken care of me since 1992

TRANSLATOR'S DEDICATION

This book is dedicated to my father,
Prof. K.N. Sundaresan (1899–1983)

When you change the way you look at things,
the things you look at change.

WAYNE DYER, American author (1940–2015)

1.

Thilakam was in a desperate hurry. 'What's wrong with you? Aren't you ready to leave?'

Amirtham, deeply engrossed in a book, raised his head and stared at her. Thilakam was very dark in complexion; why would she opt for such strong colours? She had hurriedly wrapped herself in a bright silk sari; thick patches of powder blemished her face; the sweat around the large, red dot adorning her forehead was glistening in the sweltering heat and running down to her nose.

'Why are you staring at me? We have to leave right away – we will be late for the play.' He *had* to go; Amirtham had no choice. He could admit his aversion to the theatre – after all, he knew what to expect – but what was the use? Rather, accept the truth that he was married to a wife with a poor taste in artistic values. Certainly, it was a great sacrifice on his part. The very word marriage means a mutual compromise between two souls with competing interests. That was how Thilakam would put an end to their squabbles, with a single remark, 'You are so indifferent – you hate everything I enjoy. You are like a silent Swami ji, a holy man, only interested in reading something! When you do go out with me, you act like a goat walking to a slaughterhouse! You never seem to feel you are enjoying your wife's company! Never!'

He picked up the car keys on the table. Thilakam began closing the windows and doors before leaving.

Amirtham went down and brought out the 1970-model Fiat from the shed. It was starting to lose its first sheen of newness.

'Good morning, Uncle ji!'

It was the grandchild of the Sardar ji, the Sikh gentleman, living across from their house. A plump, four-year-old child – such a sturdy and healthy child. One had a feeling she would be the top winner in every annual children's photo contest.

'Good evening, Auntie ji.'

Amirtham turned around and saw Thilakam was approaching the car. Thilakam took the child from Amirtham and hugged her hard, her cheek pressing the little one's. Poor Thilakam, she craved a child of her own. The couple had been married for twelve years, and the doctors told her she needed to have a medical procedure to conceive. Thilakam dreaded the operation so much that she wanted no children.

The child seemed out of breath in Thilakam's warm, tight embrace.

'Let her down, she's struggling,' Amirtham said.

Thilakam let her go, and the child, once free, ran to her house.

'I am barren, why do you keep reminding me?'

'Who called you barren? Stop acting like a slob – always blaming yourself for something or the other.'

Thilakam opened the car's rear door and sat down.

'Why don't you come and sit in the front?'

'I am barren, I am a slob. Let me hear you describe me in so many ways. I insist I will sit here only.'

Amirtham was in no mood to argue with her; he started the car.

In a car, the AIFACS Hall, the venue for the play, was not too far from Kidwai Nagar. Still, it was Sunday and the road outside INA Market was crowded. Their car had to wait too often for the green light to advance quickly and, finally after six, they reached their destination.

Thilakam kept grumbling the entire route, 'We should have left much earlier... This is what happens when you have no interest in accompanying me to a play. We will probably miss a complete scene.'

'So what? We can see plays whenever we want...it is no big loss,' Amirtham said. Thilakam was quiet. She seemed to be in no mood to argue with her husband. Her expression suggested her mind was fervently preoccupied with the play and nothing else mattered.

Maybe this is actually a popular play, Amirtham pondered as he watched the multitude of colourful silk saris flocking the ticket counter. There was no hope tickets would be unavailable and the couple might have to simply turn back. No such luck – Thilakam had bought them, in advance, last week.

A young man with a badge answered Thilakam and informed them the play had begun five minutes ago. When the couple went in and took their seats, a twenty-year-old woman and a man in his fifties were on the stage, enacting a love scene.

'What's going on? An old man in amorous mood?' Amirtham couldn't help asking as he settled down in his seat.

'Don't call him old. According to the story, he's only thirty years old. He also happens to be the director and hero of this play. Don't you think he deserves this privilege for being a director?'

The explanation came from a young man in a seat behind them, and others next to him joined in the laughter.

Thilakam glared at her husband.

'Stop your running commentary in a public theatre!'

That's when Amirtham looked properly at the woman on the stage.

It had been twelve years... At that instant, scenes from the past seized him.

She resembled Nitya.

There was absolutely no possible connection between her and Nitya. Nitya had married a Bengali and settled down in the United States; who was this woman?

The bright yellow rays of the stage lights lit up her face and she was smiling.

Yes, the same smile... Amirtham closed his eyes, savouring those moments. His whole body felt elated.

He had met Nitya for the last time twelve years ago.

His father had totally disregarded his son's letter, made up his mind to hold his son's wedding ceremony, chose the day and time, and announced the news by a telegram. Thilakam was Amirtham's cousin. Amirtham met Nitya in Connaught Place and told her of his father's plans for him.

'I want to send a reply – a wire – right away. I have arranged for our registered marriage. What do you say?'

Nitya was calmly engaged in cutting the cutlet on her plate; she smiled at him faintly.

'What do you say?' he repeated.

'Hmm.' She smeared some more sauce on the cutlet.

'Rome is burning, and you keep on...'

Her very composure irritated him.

'I find your talk quite funny!'

'What's funny about it?'

'Getting married isn't something that can happen at our will, immediately. I am sure my mother will never give her consent. Let's not even start on the caste considerations. And ever since I lost my father, we are beholden to my uncle; he has an only son...'

'Then, maybe we should have never started seeing one another. Were you unaware of these things before?'

'Please listen to me. Send a wire to your father that you are against this marriage. Let's wait for a while. I am not too sure if my cousin is really interested in me. He may have other ideas.'

'Are you suggesting I should wait until your cousin develops an interest in another girl? Nonsense!'

Nitya smiled. This only aggravated Amirtham even more.

'Now or never! That's my life's philosophy.'

She gave no answer. She closed her eyes and slid back against the sofa. She seemed to be enjoying herself.

'You look so happy,' Amirtham said, raising his voice. 'Finally, a sense of relief!' Her eyes still closed, Nitya gestured with her finger in the direction of the orchestra. Like the scent from an agarbatti, the music wafted in the air.

For a moment he continued to stare at her. Then, he spoke.

'I think...' he began, but could go no further.

Her eyes were still closed, but her lips moved, 'You think?'

'All this talk about your cousin is humbug. This is just a simple question of caste prejudice, that's all.'

Now she opened her eyes. Her face reddened.

'Don't. Be. Silly.' She uttered each word with force and vigour.

'Why are you so angry? Because I am speaking the truth?'

Nitya laughed, again.

'I am not angry. An accusation ought to have at least *some* merit to make one angry; yours has nothing of that kind. I am really surprised – I never imagined you harbour such an inferiority complex.'

'Okay, let's not discuss this any further. Now I know

what my message to my father ought to be. "For this relief, much thanks."'

'It's kind of funny that one quotes Shakespeare when angry,' Nitya said, and laughed.

'I can never understand you,' Amirtham said in a weary voice.

'That's my strength.'

'Damn it. You think I am one of those romantic heroes from our epics who grovel before a woman?'

'No, you are wrong! That's a Western tradition. According to our convention, it is the heroine who is supposed to cringe before the hero, his mother and grandmother!'

'Hang your traditions! All smart talk!'

Nitya stared at him. She smiled again and shrugged her shoulders. The waiter brought the bill. She took it and opened her handbag.

'What is this? A new tradition?' Amirtham asked angrily.

'I am just settling our account,' she said and closed her handbag.

After that episode, he never saw her again.

The crowd around him was now cheering.

'Why don't you laugh? Don't you like the girl's performance?'

'What girl?'

'Good heavens! Are you sleeping or watching the play?'

'I see – you are talking about the girl in the production? I don't even understand what the story is about. It looks like a surrealistic play.'

'You are so weird.' Thilakam let out a deep sigh. 'One must go with the flow.' Such an outlook would indeed lead to democratic peace and harmony.

But Amirtham never seemed to have embraced such an attitude. Nitya too had mentioned it to him many a time. Deep in his heart, he knew he could boldly venture on a trip to the moon but would feel extremely shy in the company of half-a-dozen strangers.

He recalled the day Nitya and he attended a charity ball sponsored by the US consulate. Nitya had worn a Marwari costume and within ten minutes was the life and soul of the party. She mixed freely with others and exchanged banter. As for Amirtham, he spent his entire two-hour attendance at the function sitting alone at a corner table and watching the outpouring of warmth and excitement from Nitya's presence. Nitya remained a mystery to him. She seemed capable of discussing Einstein's principles and Hoyle–Narlikar corrections; she could also infuriate loyal *Playboy* readers with her off-colour remarks.

As they were leaving, Nitya told him, 'All those folks kept on asking me about you.'

'What were they asking?'

'Why you were keenly watching my each and every movement – that's how you conducted yourself – as if spying on me from afar.'

'I remember you telling me that I don't fit in a democratic society.'

'In fact, I like your deliberate need to avoid limelight. Makes you a strong, silent man. Don't you agree?'

Nitya had reiterated this point to him often.

Was it possible she eventually got bored by this very trait of avoiding public exposure? What actually caused their minds to drift apart after that last meeting? Nitya had seen a crisis looming and she had seemed on the verge of making a final decision – but then, why did she retreat? Again, that cousin of hers – he never married Nitya. He loved some other woman and married her – it was Nitya who told Amirtham about this later. Now, Amirtham wondered: Did I act foolishly?

Yes, I was indeed a fool, there's no doubt, he concluded. Otherwise, why would he now end up sitting beside Thilakam, along with a witless crowd?

'My God, what a horror!' Thilakam screamed.

'What happened?' asked Amirtham.

'He wants to kill a baby, so he's determined to burn the entire house! Do you see how realistic the scene looks?'

Amirtham felt the author of the play should also be consigned to the flames. The villain of the piece, he thought, was not the 'evil genius' in the play, but the playwright himself. That's when that girl reappeared on the stage, her long tresses on full display, her face revealing indifference, but also a transcendent glow. She looked exactly like Nitya.

'What an excellent actress!' Thilakam exclaimed.

'Do you know her name?' Amirtham asked her.

'Who knows?' Thilakam grumbled.

'Bhanumati.' The voice came from a back row and Amirtham turned around. That voice belonged to a young woman, about twenty years old, who added, 'Bhanu is my friend.'

'I see.'

'Has she acted in any other plays?' asked Thilakam.

'No. She came to Delhi only six months ago. This is the first time she is acting in a play in the city.'

'She's very smart,' said Amirtham. A livid Thilakam stared at her husband who made no attempt to acknowledge her bruised feelings.

'Is she studying or working?' Amirtham asked.

'She's working in All India Radio.'

'You have spoken enough. Now, watch the play!' Thilakam whispered to her husband.

'You keep watching. I will wait for you outside.' Amirtham got up to leave. Thilakam grabbed his hand and pleaded, 'Do stay for a while. It should be over shortly.'

He shook off her hand and walked out.

2.

Outside the auditorium, Amirtham noticed a few drama critics from the English newspapers. Those critics made it their mission to report and review any south-Indian cultural programme happening in the city. He approached one of them, Mani, who was an acquaintance.

'Are you already leaving?' asked Mani, while chewing tobacco.

'No. My wife is inside, watching the play,' Amirtham answered.

'Well, the play is essentially meant for women. Don't you agree?' Mani remarked and laughed.

'Is that going to be in your review too?' Amirtham wanted to know.

'Yes. The Bengalis are busy setting up a new drama group every year, so they feel compelled to come up with something fresh each time. But our folks want to set up a new drama group only because they failed to get recognition and acceptance by others. As far as the theatre movement is concerned, there's nothing of note here; it is all the same story. I see no hope in the near future.'

'That happens because, I think, when it comes to judging our cultural and literary tastes, women do dominate our thinking,' said one of the men, who sported spectacles with thick frames.

'When *I* say "women", I am only talking about those with a half-baked education, who are clinging stubbornly to the establishment values,' said Amirtham.

'Well said. There's something else: when it comes to English plays, all these professors have no problem judging them fearlessly with the conventional literary yardsticks at their command. But in the case of Tamil dramas, they have no qualms watching them along with their families and children, with a sense of appreciation bordering on naïveté and total innocence! They keep raving about them; the whole thing is disgusting to me!' said Mani.

'They honestly believe they are offering their whole-hearted support to Tamil theatre,' Amirtham said. He turned.

The play was over and everyone was coming out of the auditorium.

'Mr Mani, sar! Why are you standing outside?' enquired a patron.

'I have already watched a couple of scenes, and knew exactly what I was getting into.'

'How do you like it?'

'First class. It deserves to be entered in the Commonwealth Drama Festival.'

'You really think so?'

'Yes, I mean it! I mentioned this some time ago in my column; you can check. We must not let these magnum opuses languish in our country.'

The patron left, with no more questions.

'You have to go to Moti Bagh, don't you? I can drop you at your place,' Amirtham told Mani.

'No, thanks. I have come on my scooter,' Mani told him.

'You missed so much. It was a great play!' Thilakam said, as she came up and joined her husband.

'Do you hear what she's saying?' Mani asked with a touch of sarcasm in his voice. 'How can we deny the pleasure to the majority of the patrons? I am leaving now.'

'I am thirsty. Can I get some water to drink?' asked Thilakam.

'Let's go and have some Coca Cola there.'

'How could you go calling that woman "smart", when I was sitting beside you? Were you dreaming? Do you think you have regained your youth?' Thilakam asked him while sipping the Coca Cola.

'Such behaviour would be unacceptable in one's youth. Now, I am enjoying the privilege of age.'

'You are not yet old enough to claim that privilege,' she reminded him. 'You better be careful. When a man reaches forty, they say, he acts like a dog whose leash may just have to be yanked to stop him from chasing after the slightest distraction or temptation that comes along the way.'

Five or more persons – including three women – were standing nearby. They must have clearly heard her, for they suddenly stopped talking, turned around and looked at Thilakam, much to her husband's dismay. Hastily, Amirtham deposited cash at the counter and walked away.

'Our folks are always snooping around!' Thilakam scoffed and scurried to catch up with him.

'You keep hollering so that everybody can hear you! You expect them to close their ears?' Amirtham growled.

'You always keep blaming me – one way or the other. You don't want to go out with me. You always find an excuse to say something to contradict me!'

Amirtham was averse to prolonging their argument; he could never predict when Thilakam would explode in public, and should that happen, their private struggle would turn into a street brawl.

Approaching his car, Amirtham noticed his friend Balu, with three other men, standing with the woman who had acted in the play.

'Hello – here comes Mr Amirtham. Let's ask

him,' Balu was telling them. He turned to Amirtham and smiled.

'Hello, what do you need?' asked Amirtham.

'You are going to Kidwai Nagar. Can you drop off this girl in Lakshmibai Nagar? She needs to go right away – her mother is sick. She came down here only because she consented to act in the play.'

Amirtham noticed the badge on Balu's shirt.

'So, you are also associated with this drama troupe?' Amirtham asked.

'I am the vice president!' Balu replied proudly..

'I see. I can take her.'

'You may get in,' Balu urged the woman.

Amirtham opened the rear door and she got in.

'Thanks, Mr Amirtham. Bhanu, I will see you later.'

Smiling, Bhanu nodded her head towards Balu in acknowledgement.

Thilakam sat down in the front seat, next to Amirtham. She banged the car door hard, and he jumped a little. Her studied silence annoyed him. Was she displeased because he was readily willing to give the woman a ride?

'Take it easy,' he told her in a whisper.

He was a little surprised when she did not reply.

Everyone in the car was silent until it travelled past the Great Place, when Bhanu asked politely, using the honorific 'Aunt' for an older woman, 'Mami, how did you like the play?'

'Hmm. You mean the play? It was good.'

'Did you like it?' Bhanu asked Amirtham.

'Well, he never bothered to watch it. He seemed angry and in a bad mood,' Thilakam said.

'The drama was hopeless, but you acted very well!' Amirtham told her.

'Why didn't you take off your make-up? Are you in such a hurry?' Thilakam asked.

'Yes, Mother is very sick. She's at home, alone.'

'What does your father do?' asked Amirtham.

'My father is no more. You are right. I acted in the play only to keep my word. The play is very childish.'

She's indeed smart, Amirtham thought. She gives a

brief answer and then tries to turn the conversation in a different direction.

'My husband says the story is hopeless. You are calling it childish. Then why did you promise to act in it?'

'Well, sometimes we do what goes against the grain, don't we? Let's say this is one of those instances.'

'What do you mean by "going against the grain"?' asked Amirtham.

Bhanu was quiet for a while. Then, she laughed and asked, 'Can I ask you something? I am only hoping...'

'What are you hoping?' asked Amirtham.

'... that you won't get angry with me.'

Amirtham couldn't imagine what she might ask him. Why take the risk of letting Bhanu speak her piece and possibly hurt Thilakam's sentiments?

'He won't be angry; go ahead – ask!' Thilakam urged her.

'You consider the play hopeless. I think this is something you had known all along. Then, why did you want to see it?'

'I asked him to come, so he did,' Thilakam answered

in a conceited voice. Amirtham switched on the car's interior light. He looked through the rear mirror. Bhanu was smiling; was it a mark of indifference born out of self-confidence?

Suddenly, a strange feeling seized him: Was it Nitya sitting in the rear seat, laughing at him? He recalled a conversation he and Nitya once had on what is 'aesthetic sense'.

Nitya insisted they both visit a roadside eatery near the Red Fort and enjoy chholey. The idea was so laughable to Amirtham that he howled, 'Oh my God! *That's* what you really want to do?'

'I don't know much about your taste in general, but you totally lack imagination,' Nitya told him. 'Just imagine how the Red Fort could serve as an excellent backdrop.'

'Okay, go ahead and eat. I will not.'

Amirtham recalled that episode. What would Nitya say *now*? 'You were harping on the word "aesthetics" all the time. How come finally you selected this woman as your life partner? Oh, I am sorry – your wife must have selected you, am I right?'

Amirtham switched off the car lights.

'Why are you switching the lights on and off?' asked Thilakam.

'We keep doing many useless things. This is one of them,' Amirtham said. Bhanu laughed. He thought she laughed a bit too hard.

'I don't find anything funny in your answer,' Thilakam said.

'I too feel the same way,' Amirtham said.

'I like the way Mami speaks – she's very frank,' Bhanu said.

'Does it mean I am not being open and direct when I speak?' asked Amirtham.

'I have no firm opinion on that matter.'

Amirtham thought of switching on the lights again and looking at her, but he didn't. Under these circumstances, Nitya too would be talking like Bhanu.

Then he recalled something else. His friend Kesavan, who belonged to this drama troupe, had probably referred to Bhanu in a conversation. 'We now have a new girl from Madras. What an incredible actress! Her mother is also an actress, but this daughter is simply unbelievable!' If so, why didn't the mother show up? He remembered now: *She's sick.* How soon he forgot!

'Your mother also acts in plays, am I right?' asked Amirtham.

'She does. How do you know that? She too was supposed to act in this play, but she fell sick. Now, who told you my mother is an actress?'

'I heard from someone.'

'Who told you? You never told me,' Thilakam said.

Amirtham was silent. The car passed through Tughlaq Road. Suddenly, a teenager on a bicycle, coming from the opposite direction, swerved and brushed against the vehicle, and fell on the road. Amirtham hit the brakes and brought the car to a stop so suddenly that Thilakam dashed against her husband.

Amirtham got out of the car and patted down the teenager who seemed badly shaken. Fortunately, the bicycle showed no damage and the boy too was unhurt.

'*Maaf karoji*,' the boy said.

'*Theek hai, chalo.*'

Back in the car, as they drove on, Thilakam started to admonish her husband, 'How come you were sweet-talking that boy? You should have slapped him hard.'

'Poor little fellow, wasn't he scared enough?'

'You are always considerate to others. Why don't you have the same concern for me?'

What was Thilakam hinting at? Was it because Amirtham agreed to drop Bhanu home?

'You have still not answered my question,' Thilakam said.

'What question, what concern?'

'That's what I want to know! Besides, who told you her mother also acts in plays? How come you never told me?'

'Impossible! Do you expect me to tell you everything I come to know?'

Amirtham could feel his wife glaring at him, but he did not look at her. The car sped beyond the Safdarjung airport, and Amirtham stopped at a red light near a traffic junction leading to Lakshmibai Nagar.

'If Lakshmibai Nagar is the destination, this is where you get off,' Thilakam said. It was obvious that she didn't want Amirtham to drop off Bhanu at her home.

'Okay, let me get down here,' Bhanu said. 'My house is close by, within walking distance.'

'Don't get off yet. Tell me the block number, I can drop you there.'

'No, I don't want to give you extra trouble. From here you can go to Kidwai Nagar straight.'

'Stop arguing. What's the block number? Tell me quick! The light has turned green. Don't worry about our inconvenience.'

Bhanu was still hesitant. Did she expect Thilakam to utter those words instead? Amirtham was annoyed.

'Tell me, quick; I can't stop here forever!'

'Take a left and go straight. C-block, house number 65.'

He steered the car to the left. A bus came close, ready to hit them; he avoided collision by a hair's breadth.

'I think you're too excited to know what you're doing,' said Thilakam.

'Don't be silly.' Amirtham tightened his grip on the steering wheel.

'Please stop right here,' Bhanu told him.

Bhanu got out of the car and formally took leave of Thilakam with a smile.

'Mami, many thanks! It's very late or I would have invited you into the house.'

'Don't bother,' said Thilakam.

'Bye, Mama.'

Amirtham felt a little odd to be addressed as Mama. He silently steered the car. Thilakam laughed. Amirtham had been thinking all along she had been in an angry mood, so her laughter surprised him. He turned around and looked at her.

'She did the proper thing in calling you Mama; aren't you past forty?'

'When you have turned into Mami, it is quite logical I am Mama. What is funny about it?'

'Don't get mad at turning older. We do get old – whether we like it or not.'

Amirtham could make no sense of her new attack. He became quiet and remained silent until they reached home.

3.

Once they were home, he jumped on her, 'I have never seen an idiot like you. You have been complaining all the way. What will that girl think of you?'

'How does that matter? I don't live for others.'

'All right, all right,' Amirtham mumbled to himself and slumped on a nearby sofa, clasping his hands behind his head.

'I have never seen you hollering like this before. Why are you so upset *today*?'

Amirtham closed his eyes.

Sleep eluded him that night. Why this change in Thilakam? She had gauged his reactions perfectly today – normally, she was never sensitive to the feelings of people around her. Her friendships with anyone never lasted more than two days. She had turned bitter and cynical because she had not been blessed with motherhood even after twelve years of marriage. Amirtham had stopped arguing with her and had been leading a mechanical life. How long could he go on with this artificial life? Yet...what Thilakam had said was embarrassingly true.

Amirtham had never mentioned anything about Nitya to Thilakam. Thilakam was stuck with a notion that her cousin Amirtham had always been destined to marry her, only her. Such was her obsession that Thilakam seemed trapped inside a narrow circle where she lacked both the imagination and desire to think of anything other than her husband. Amirtham had been averse to talk about Nitya to Thilakam. He believed it to be the best favour he could offer his wife. Now he had a sudden thought: Should I tell her? He turned around and looked at her.

Thilakam was fast asleep. One could call her neither ugly nor beautiful. She had grown up with an authoritarian streak and seemed all wound up, but her sloppiness was very evident. She was childless; maybe that was the reason her face betrayed a childlike innocence. Perhaps that was the price for not becoming a mother.

Nitya was a real beauty. It was his misfortune that Amirtham could never forget her. Like a thorn, her memory, from deep inside, continued to pierce his heart.

He recalled the scene when Bhanu took leave of Thilakam: the girl's head slightly bent down, the row of upper teeth enmeshing with the lower lip as she spoke. That was when she looked exactly like Nitya. How Amirtham wished all the twelve years he had lived so far had been a dream. He savoured those moments and found some comfort in those thoughts. Then he heard Thilakam snoring lightly in her sleep.

He got out of bed and walked to the veranda. Darkness swept all around him. Heavy silence hovered over the surroundings. Afar, he watched the Ring Road encircling Delhi. A row of hospital buildings caught his attention. Who knows how many patients occupying them were struggling with their private ailments and agonies? They remained invisible to the outside world while those staid buildings stood in silence against the majestic sky.

'What are you doing there?'

Thilakam must have awakened; her voice broke the prevailing quietude. Amirtham closed the veranda door and retreated into the house.

'I couldn't sleep. I was just standing there.'

'Who's on your mind?' She was half asleep and lay on the bed, her face turned towards the wall. But the rancour in her voice reached Amirtham.

He sat on the bed.

'Do you want to know?'

'Know what?'

'Who's on my mind?'

'If you tell me you were thinking about me, that would be a bald lie!'

'It was not you.'

'Then, who was it?' She turned towards him. Her sleep was gone. This was bound to happen some day, anyway.

'Before I married you, I was friendly with another woman. And I was thinking about her.' He felt calm and resolute as he uttered those words.

'Really?' Thilakam sat up on the bed.

'Presently I am not in a mood to tell any lies.'

'Please turn the switch and make the fan go faster. I feel very stuffy.'

If she felt the atmosphere stifling in late October, one could be sure it had nothing to do with her body.

Amirtham let the fan whirl faster. 'Do you need the light?'

She shook her head, saying no. Amirtham glanced at the clock on the table. The luminous dial indicated three.

'I was always proud of you – on this particular matter. Now, that too is gone.'

'What matter are you talking about?'

'That you weren't involved with another woman.'

'I am not responsible for what you think.'

'Why didn't you tell me this before?'

'What do you mean by "before"?'

'I mean, as soon as we got married.'

'Had I told you, what would you have done?'

'All these days I have been cherishing a false idea of you. Now, I have suddenly come to know that I have been cheated! Can't you understand how that betrayal would upset me?'

Amirtham hadn't expected this rejoinder. He thought she would make her feelings known by crying aloud and raising hell. He was quite taken aback by Thilakam's vulnerability.

'Who's she?' she asked. He was a little frightened by the calmness in her voice.

'She's not here. She has moved to the States. After the wedding, I haven't seen her.'

'After whose wedding?'

'After our wedding. Come on, stop acting like a lawyer! Why do you keep cross-examining me?'

Thilakam got down from the bed and walked to the veranda.

'Was that the reason you have been so aloof?'

'No, that has nothing to do with this! I have told you, I have not seen her after we got married! You keep imagining all kinds of things.'

'What if you have not seen her? You have been thinking about her all the time. That's a betrayal.'

Amirtham slid back onto the bed.

'Go back to sleep. No need to fight at night.'

'Why did you think of her today?'

Amirtham was silent.

'Shall I tell you?' Thilakam snarled.

'Tell me what?' Seated on the bed, he turned to her.

'Remember that girl, Bhanu, you dropped off this evening at her home? Her mother was your ex-lover. You got so outraged when I asked you how you knew she acted in plays. Now I understand everything.'

'Stop it! You are talking rubbish.'

'Why are you mad at me? Your conscience knows I am speaking the truth. You say she is living in America or Australia – that's a lie!'

Amirtham didn't know how to respond. The more she argued, the angrier he became, and his body shuddered.

He opened the door and walked out. He had never been this angry.

What made him so mad? Was it because Thilakam accused him of an imaginary crime? Bhanu might be twenty or twenty-two at the most, so her mother couldn't be less than forty. Was he furious with himself when Thilakam linked him with Bhanu's mother? Anyway, what was the girl's crime, when she addressed him as Mama? Amirtham grumbled, 'And there's no one to exchange one's life with, either, like Puru did with his father Yayati.' Yayati was a character in the Mahabharata who was cursed by his father-in-law to age prematurely. He was told he could use the years of someone else's life, if they were willing, and his son Puru gave up his years to him.

Youth is such a blissful period! He recalled the first time he met Nitya at Regal theatre. He had seen the movie *Three Coins in a Fountain* and was returning home when he saw her near a bus stop. He knew her slightly; he knew she lived with her mother in Karol Bagh, on the first floor of the house where he himself had lived once.

At the time he had a scooter. He wanted to give her a ride. He approached her and she accepted, after some hesitation.

He was a dashing young man, so Nitya seemed slightly timid.

Today, Bhanu had shown no such qualms whatsoever and had been willing to ride with him in his car. That was because of her total trust in him. Why didn't she reveal some uncertainty? Amirtham now thought, and then told himself: What a foolish idea! Why would she waver when Thilakam was present?

That day, when he dropped Nitya home, she invited him to her flat on the first floor. He didn't want to refuse but he was concerned about how her mother would feel. But as soon as Nitya introduced him to her mother at the front door, the woman warmly welcomed him into the house.

'Had she waited for the bus, she would be home only around ten,' she said. Amirtham thought it was a very progressive family. After Nitya's father's death, the family came under the care of her uncle. At the time, her mother had only passed her Intermediate. She completed her MA in Home Science and was now working in a Delhi college.

'You can have your dinner here. You might as well miss your mess meal tonight,' Nitya's mother said, referring to the dining hall attached to the quarters where unmarried officers lived.

'Oh, no, don't trouble yourself,' Amirtham said and tried to leave.

'No, no. You talk to Nitya. Dinner will be ready in a minute.'

That 'minute' turned to half an hour. But it seemed only a minute because he was talking to Nitya. Nitya worked as a receptionist in an office. She said she had run into Amirtham many a time and had wanted to talk with him. Amirtham was pleasantly surprised and responded awkwardly, saying, 'I am a cog in the government's vast bureaucratic machine!' provoking loud laughter from her. He loved that. Her hobby was photography. She showed him several photographs in her album.

'I have no particular hobby,' Amirtham confessed to her. 'I believe I am aesthetically inclined – I admire the beautiful things I see and hear.' Her face reddened.

That night, after dinner, he returned home around eleven.

What a difference! Tonight felt poles apart from the one when Amirtham dropped Nitya off at her home.

Is life just an effort to meditate on past events and dreams? Had his dreams of that night materialized, Amirtham wouldn't be stuck here tonight, standing on the veranda and chewing over bygone days. Past events inflict the harshest punishment to one's memory. The happiest thing about memory is that one's dream remains a dream forever! Don't things look more beautiful when observed through a kaleidoscope rather than when seen directly?

His life of the past twelve years had been a veritable lie. All the while he had been leading a phony life – barely fashioned out of the moral values dictated by his conscience. He was averse to go against the social mores and thus lived in a comfort zone, nurturing a herd instinct. All he wanted was peace of mind: so, feeling essentially helpless, he sought compromise. Must his life end like this?

Then he heard Thilakam sobbing. I am the one who deserves to cry, Amirtham wondered, why is *she* weeping?

4.

Thilakam had erected a wall of silence around herself. Amirtham was averse to breach it. Thus, a week went by with continued stillness between the couple.

It was the second Saturday of the month. The All-India Art Exhibition was going on at the Rabindra Bhavan and Amirtham wanted to go. Should he ask Thilakam to accompany him? He knew she had no interest in art exhibitions, but if she found out that her husband had gone to the show without asking her, it was most likely this ongoing silence between the couple would never cease; the next two days would be a torture.

He asked her while she served him lunch, 'I am thinking of going to the art exhibition.'

'I am not coming,' Thilakam said as she placed a bowl of curd on the table.

'You can come – if you are interested.'

'I am not coming.'

Amirtham was a little excited that she had refused his offer. At the same time, he also felt a little compassion for her.

After lunch, he got ready to leave for the exhibition. When he was seated in the car, he became aware that she was watching him from a window upstairs.

Did she expect he would ask her again? Maybe she would accept and join him, who knew? Amirtham avoided her eyes and started the car.

It was publicized as an all-India exhibition, but not many states had sent in their art for display. Political intrusion and mischief had corrupted the art world so deeply that many artists withheld their cooperation. It was the central government that sponsored this exhibition; yet, the artists looked down upon the members of the selection committee and felt them inept to judge their works. Except for a few notable exceptions, most of the pieces of art in the exhibition were of an average quality.

One of the paintings, titled 'Deluge', stood apart from the rest. To Amirtham's eyes, it was an amazing display – a sudden confluence of colours. Its artist had another painting on display, which seemed very mundane. In 'Deluge', the colours themselves, independent of the theme and form, dominated and touched the viewer's heart. Here was a work of art that conveyed Mother Nature at work in concrete physical terms. Amirtham stared at the painting, mesmerized.

The artist of that painting was not well known. Yet, Amirtham concluded, the artist too must have experienced the turmoil and travail he was himself now enduring.

'Namaskaram.'

He turned around. It was Bhanu, her slender body draped in a bright-red nylon sari and a black blouse. She smiled and her eyes lit up as well.

'I am in awe,' he said.

'Why?'

Amirtham realized he had blurted out something weird in his present state of mind, but was in no hurry to offer any explanation.

'This is a great painting!' he said and continued to stare at it.

'It is a good painting.'

'Why only such a simple approval?'

'The simplest explanation is the best tribute. Everything else is just wasting words.'

Amirtham smiled at her.

'You are talking like a real connoisseur of art!'

'No, please! I am not a critic.'

'I am not attacking you! Please don't refuse my compliment!'

Bhanu laughed again, and dimples appeared in her cheeks.

'How do you like the exhibition?' she asked.

'So-so, like all the government exhibitions.'

'You too belong to the government, don't you?'

'How do you know?'

'If you live in Kidwai Nagar, that clearly says you are a government servant.' Was she checking on his whereabouts? The very idea disappointed him. Bhanu tried to cheer him up.

'I am not attacking you.'

Amirtham laughed.

They both walked out of Rabindra Bhavan.

'Going home?' Amirtham asked her.

'Yes,' she said, adding, 'thanks,' in answer to his next question.

'I too do some painting – oil painting,' Bhanu said, once she was inside the car.

'You do? I want to see them!'

'There's not a lot. What about you?'

'I am no artist – I am just an admirer. To what school of art do you belong?'

'I belong to no school. I just follow my instinct.'

'That makes you a free spirit. If you belong to a particular school, you are forever caught up in a trap with no chance of escape.'

The car was travelling on Feroz Shah Road. While crossing Curzon Road, as many Delhiites still referred to Kasturba Gandhi Marg, a fast-approaching autorickshaw almost dashed against the car.

Amirtham deftly avoided the accident and stopped the vehicle.

'Whenever we happen to meet, I seem to get involved in an accident!' Amirtham said and laughed.

'I believe your overwhelming excitement could be a reason.'

Apparently, she had not forgotten what Thilakam had remarked the other day.

'You have a good memory.'

'It's the only thing that makes life interesting.'

How true! Bhanu was also just like Nitya, who, like Amirtham, had an opinion on everything under the sun.

He met Nitya a second time just a week after their first meeting. There she was, in an ice cream parlour, her hands holding several New Year greeting cards.

'Hello!'

'Come, sit. You too can have some ice cream!' She ordered the waiter to bring coffee, too.

'Thanks. You don't seem to worry too much about your weight.'

'I think I am too thin. I really want to gain a few pounds.'

'Then, have some more.'

'Okay.'

He was a little surprised she accepted his suggestion immediately.

'You seem to have a lot of friends,' Amirtham said as he glanced at the greeting cards in her hand.

'Yes. You might be getting one, too.'

'Thanks. That means I too should buy one this year.'

'Does it mean you have only one friend?'

He nodded his head in assent.

'You are nodding your head as if you are proud of it.'

'Proud about what? That I have only one friend? Well, yes.'

She gave no reply. As the silence lengthened, Amirtham worried that he had talked too much.

'I like your mother,' he said as a way of toning things down.

'My mother likes you too.'

Was it a subtle warning that Amirtham must safeguard his reputation with her mother? Why else would she say that? The mere thought thrilled his heart.

'I knew even then that you don't have friends,' he said.

'When?'

'The day I saw you in a movie theatre. At your age, who goes to the movies alone?'

'What about you? Didn't you go alone?'

'Well... A bachelor goes to a movie *alone*; an unmarried woman goes to a movie *with* someone.

Two separate events – but both demand careful explanations!'

'You talk like Oscar Wilde.'

'I take it as a compliment.'

They reached her home.

'I want you to visit my little abode,' Amirtham said.

'Please wait – let me have a word with my mom,' Nitya said and went upstairs. She returned after a while; Amirtham noticed she had changed her clothes.

She stood before the bookshelf and started examining Amirtham's library in his apartment.

Amirtham stood beside her as the fragrance from the flowers adorning her tresses filled his heart. When Nitya tried to reach for a book a little too high up for her, Amirtham preempted her and took it out even as his body swayed and came in direct contact with hers. Nitya stood there, leafing through its pages. Later, she said, 'Please return it to its place.' Amirtham, once again, brushed his body against her. Nitya must have known this was no mere accident. Yet, she stood right there, steady and silent.

And on that day, Amirtham fully grasped the meaning of silence.

Nitya took leave of him after half an hour. Amirtham came to know that her mother had not been home all that day. This revelation came from Nitya herself on another occasion.

'Do you not talk while driving?' asked Bhanu.

'No. I was just thinking what you said about memory being a very interesting thing.'

'Looks like you have a lot of things to think about.'

'Yes... There's a lot.'

Bhanu stared at him and fell silent.

'Are you thinking what I am thinking?' asked Amirtham.

She gave no reply, and laughed. After a while she asked him, 'Remember, that day you gave no answer to a question I asked. Can you answer it today?'

'What's the question?'

'Who told you my mother used to act in theatre?'

'My friend Kesavan. He said, "The daughter and mother brought star value to our theatre group."'

'Star value? You must be joking.' Bhanu pushed her

flowing hair forward and adjusted the ribbon at its tip. Her coldness upset Amirtham – was she stroking his bruised ego with a flippant, feminine gesture?

'You are a versatile artist – well versed in many arts – acting, painting... Do you dance, too?'

'Yes, a little. Mother was known as a good dancer, too. She has performed in Madras in the good old days.'

'Did your family originally belong to Madras?'

'No, we belonged to Tiruvarur. Father was a teacher there.'

'So, he moved to Madras?"

'Why do you keep talking about the past? Why don't you ask me what I am doing *now*?' Amirtham realized she was in no mood to answer his question.

5.

'I am sorry. I am not trying to pry into your personal life,' Amirtham protested.

'That's all right. Now my mother runs a dance school; I am working in AIR. We came to Delhi a year ago.'

'You are lucky! You got the quarters allotment immediately after your arrival.'

Bhanu laughed.

'Why do you laugh?'

'I am a little surprised you talk like a typical government employee.'

Amirtham felt humiliated. Twelve years ago, he would have never spoken like that. As a bachelor, when he was having his meals in a mess, he would easily get irritated when his colleagues discussed increment confirmations and promotion rules. These folks are easily pleased; everyone among them has dedicated his entire life to the government, he would muse. Bhanu's words now hit him like a slap on the face.

'I am getting old.'

'What?'

'I am getting old, so I am talking about allotment, retirement and such things. One needs security, don't you agree?'

Amirtham spoke because he felt sorry for himself. Bhanu was silent. He expected she would protest against his remark about old age, but her silence disappointed him.

'I didn't answer your question about my father moving to Madras – and you didn't ask me why,' said Bhanu.

'You were expecting I would ask?'

'As a matter of fact, no. But now I feel like answering that question.'

Amirtham was quiet.

Bhanu continued, 'My parents didn't get along well with one another. After they got married, my father was totally against my mother performing dances in public. So my mother came down to Madras with me.'

The car reached Lakshmibai Nagar. Amirtham stopped the car at a corner.

'Aren't you a little surprised that I am talking to you like this – the second time we are seeing one another?'

'In fact, no.' Bhanu smiled.

'Can I ask you a question?' Amirtham asked.

'Go ahead.'

'Where do your sympathies lie? With your mother or father?'

'With Father. I hate Mother – I detest her!' The natural laughter in her eyes suddenly disappeared as she stared out through the windscreen. Her jaw tightened; it was clear it was no lie when she spoke of her revulsion for her mother.

'Where's your father?'

'Till the end, he stayed in Tiruvarur; he has been dead for over five years.'

'When was the last time you saw him?'

'I haven't seen him since I moved to Madras with Mother. The last time I saw him I was only six.'

'Excuse me... but at six you could have hardly known your father well, so how can you say your sympathies are with him? How do you know how he treated your mother?'

'I have been living with my mother for many years, so I can certainly imagine how she would have treated him. Don't you agree?'

'You really are very smart,' Amirtham said.

'Enough. Stop praising me! I am not saying all this to prove how smart I am. I want to get away from my mother; I don't know what to do.'

Bhanu said it in such a calm, measured tone that Amirtham was taken aback. Her sombre voice suggested she must have deliberated this for many years before arriving at this decision.

'Is it such a simple matter – to throw away one's relationship?'

'My mother dared. Why can't I?'

'I think we have covered a lot for the second day,' said Amirtham.

'It is getting late for you, am I right?' Bhanu opened the car door.

'No...what I meant was – today I talked with you openly about several things.' Bhanu got out.

'Do you want to come in?' she asked.

Amirtham hesitated.

'Don't be concerned about what I said about my mother. Please come in. Don't you want to see my paintings?'

'Oh, I forgot.' Amirtham got out of the car.

'Your wife was not too happy the other day when you dropped me home; am I right?'

'Yes, that's true.'

'That's what I thought... By the way, how many children do you have?'

'Why "by the way"?' Amirtham answered her, smiling. 'You can ask me directly. I have no children. Don't tell me, again, "That's what I thought." That would be cruel!'

Bhanu pressed the doorbell and her mother opened the door. She seemed a little confused on seeing Amirtham.

'Please come in,' Bhanu said.

They went in. Bhanu introduced Amirtham to her mother Janaki. Amirtham was a little surprised when Bhanu told her he was a deputy secretary in the Health Ministry. He realized Bhanu had made enquiries about him.

He could see Janaki must have once been a great beauty.

'I'll be back,' Bhanu said and went in.

Janaki gestured to Amirtham to take a nearby chair. He was a little surprised that Janaki's make-up, even at home, bordered on extravagance. The eyes conveyed dominance, the face brought to light an artist's fame and popularity as a dancer. Her smile could attract any man at first sight. Amirtham tried to imagine how she would have looked in her youth; how this beauty could have let herself be confined to the narrow circle of Tiruvarur – that too with a schoolteacher. She wanted to explore new horizons, so her first act was to move to a big city like Madras.

It was not surprising that Bhanu's relationship with her mother was fraught. Maybe Bhanu saw herself as her father's daughter. Any woman who hates her mother – the parent who is physically visible to her all the time – must be fixated on her absent father; it was natural she felt more secure in seeking a father figure.

Bhanu served him coffee.

'Oh, thank you. What about the paintings?'

'Don't I need to bribe you to win your approval? So, I am serving you coffee first!'

Amirtham took a sip.

'Now that I have enjoyed the coffee, it would be a sin to dislike your paintings – even if they are awful.'

'I see! So, what you are saying about the coffee – is it a truth or a lie?' asked Bhanu.

'Our coffee powder is not good enough, so how can you expect good taste?' Janaki said.

'I disagree. The coffee is really A-one!'

As he spoke, Amirtham leafed through a concert programme on a nearby table. He noticed Janaki's photo in it. The name was Janaki Ramachandran; the programme had been published for her dance performance in Karol Bagh.

'How did you get to know Bhanu?' Janaki asked.

'The other day I went to see a play. I gave her a ride back here in my car. Didn't Bhanu tell you?'

'No. Where do you live?'

'Kidwai Nagar.'

'That's not too far from here. Do you live with your family?'

'Me and my wife only. No children.'

'Have you been only recently married?'

Amirtham laughed.

'Do I look like someone recently married? I have been married for twelve years.'

'Is that so?'

Amirtham could discern from the tone that her astonishment was a pretence. Meanwhile, Bhanu brought out her paintings.

'Oh, your paintings?' Janaki exclaimed in a tone that was a blend of pride and teasing. Some of the paintings were better than average.

'You do seem to have an artistic flair,' Amirtham complimented her.

'Really? Thank you!' Bhanu responded.

'The coffee as well as the opportunity to see these paintings – both are good bribes.'

'Why should I bribe you?' Bhanu asked.

'I don't know.' He shrugged his shoulders and arose.

'Oh, are you leaving?' Janaki asked.

'Yes, it is getting late.'

'Do visit us again with your wife.'

Bhanu walked with him to his car.

'When can I see you again?'

Bhanu gave no reply.

'Tomorrow is Sunday. Can we meet in the evening?'

Again, she gave no reply.

'Sorry, if you are not willing–'

Bhanu interrupted him, 'I will call you. What's your home phone number?' He gave it to her. She recited it twice to herself.

'Ta-ta. Goodbye!'

Bhanu stood there watching till the car reached the end of Lakshmibai Nagar and disappeared from her view.

Suddenly Amirtham was thrilled, as if he had turned twelve years younger. But could he physically rise to the occasion and cope with the challenges arising out of his new thinking?

This is a test – a welcome change to my monotonous life, he thought.

But what if he was simply wrong? It could be a figment of his imagination that Bhanu was yet another version of Nitya...

When he reached home, it was drowning in darkness. On opening the door, in the dim light from the street, he noticed Thilakam's unkempt hair and guessed she must have been resting in the bedroom. He switched on the light. *The Hindu*, the newspaper delivered that evening, lay on the table. He picked it up and went out to the balcony.

Thilakam brought him a cup of coffee and set it on a table.

'I don't want coffee.'

She took back the coffee and was gone. Her silence irritated him, but he couldn't understand why.

Soon the bedroom light went out. He assumed Thilakam had gone to bed.

What's wrong with Thilakam? he wondered. Was she harbouring a foolish notion that there was no room for attractiveness in life after a woman got married? Once she turned thirty, Thilakam had mentally groomed herself for a life of old age; she was naïve enough to stubbornly think that neither she nor her husband could have individual lives. Now, what made her act as if there was a disaster in the making? Like Queen Kaikeyi in the Ramayana, who, with her messy and tousled hair, was expecting boons, Thilakam too was up to playing tricks. The darkness around Amirtham aggravated the emptiness in his heart.

From below, the sounds of the frolicking children began to fade away. The sense of isolation in his own house, the darkness hovering over him and his silent acquiescence to the thoughts crowding his mind, lured him into the days of his youth.

His home was on Nageswaran Temple Sannathi Street in Kumbakonam. Two young sisters, both widows, lived in a house across the street. The house was quite big, like a mansion, and invariably the house would go dark around seven in the evening. At the time, Amirtham was fifteen or sixteen.

One day he asked them, 'Why do you go to sleep so early?'

The younger one told him, 'We eat, we sleep, we awake; we eat, we sleep, we awake... That's what we are fated to do, day after day! We keep on doing this and soon our life will be over! Why does this house need a light?'

Are humans destined to follow life dictated by calendars? Are we born to live our days only awaiting death? Is life a long rehearsal where one prepares for death? It is only when we consider birth as an accident and death as an inescapable truth, do we think of finding a rationale to live our life. The apple in the Garden of Eden and the one that Newton noticed falling on the ground were the same. This is pure common sense but we indulge in self-deception by calling it evil.

Amirtham couldn't concentrate on the newspaper. He got up and went in.

Should he switch on the light? No, that would mean he was condoning Thilakam's action. There was enough light to see.

Thilakam turned around in the bed to face him. She must have been crying; her face looked swollen. Their eyes met and wavered.

'Why are you this late?' Her words rose up from the edge of darkness, the agonized voice suspended in the stifling air, reminding him of the twelve years of their marriage.

He stood there, silent. Should he answer her? He didn't want to lie. In his present mood, he found no reason to lie.

'Remember her – that woman, Bhanu? I visited her today.'

Suddenly Thilakam arose, as if she had been expecting this very answer.

6.

‘How could you get this crazy?’ she sneered. Amirtham stood silently near the bed as if he had anticipated this very rebuke from her.

‘I knew it! Her mere look told me everything!’

The anger in her face grew even more intense, as her eyes and lips trembled; her rather large body shook a little.

‘Why did you come back? You could have stayed right there!’

‘Only now I realize I made a mistake.’

‘What did you say? You made a mistake? What did you say?’ Thilakam got off the bed and shook him.

He had never seen her this angry. She was furious, like a wild animal on guard. Her voice conveyed her pent-up emotions: the frustration of being childless after twelve years of marriage; the dread that her husband would feel tired and exhausted of her; and now, he was openly admitting what she had long suspected. After yanking him, Thilakam covered her eyes tightly with both hands and, in the same posture, she disappeared into another room, and shut the door behind her.

A wild storm had come to an end. His life, still and inert, would change dramatically – it would do them both good, Amirtham hoped. There would be no more room for phony values imposed upon them as a husband and wife; here was an opportunity for the couple to see one another clearly.

Still, he couldn't help wondering – would Thilakam understand the situation if she indulged in some serious thinking? No, she would never fathom how much she had grown weary of her husband. Even if she tried, she would not understand, and would only acquiesce. Should she concede, what would happen to the hallowed Indian tradition?

Amirtham could have easily hidden the truth from her; he could have asserted that he had never loved any woman other than Thilakam – thus conferring a reputation to a lie and deceiving her. Thilakam might know it was a lie, yet she would enjoy peace of mind, and seek relief and security in his company. Still, where was the need for *him* to lie?

He took off his shoes and, without changing, lay on the bed.

How could he explain his involvement with Bhanu? Was it because she reminded him of Nitya? Or was it because such a remembrance revived the sweet dreams of his youth, the memories adding flavour to his thoughts?

Could he relive the past? Amirtham recognized his thoughts and feelings – to recreate and experience again those bygone days – were unique to him, his character and personality. Could he regain all of them? Did he now have the audacity to relive each precious moment of his former days?

Once, he and Nitya were visiting Humayun's mausoleum. It was a sunny afternoon in March when the pair toured the tomb and its surroundings. There was Nitya, one hand clutching the loose end of her sari against the breeze while the other pushed back the tresses falling on her face.

'These Mughal emperors seem desperately eager to live on in history,' said Nitya.

'That desperation has actually transformed into great architecture,' Amirtham told her.

'Humayun was a colourless emperor, yet he gets such a beautiful mausoleum!'

'What do you mean? He might have been colourless. Yet, he was in the throes of death, survived it, became an emperor and won battles. His entire life was like an exciting, fast-moving drama! He had a survival instinct, unique to himself.'

'Why talk only about Humayun? Everyone has the survival instinct, it's a biological fact.'

'Biological fact? Now, that reminds me – Nitya, I love you!'

'Shut up,' she chided him.

Beneath the main burial chamber and surrounding it were several mini chambers with smaller tombs. Amirtham and Nitya visited every one of them.

'So many tombs! Who even are these people?' asked Nitya.

'Don't you know? A Mughal emperor's harem would have close to six hundred women.'

'I sense a little jealousy in your voice,' Nitya said and pinched his ear.

He laughed.

Nitya was leading Amirtham into one of the rooms, when suddenly, she hastily retreated, pushing him behind her. She looked as though she had had a shock.

'What? What happened? Why this hurry?' Amirtham asked her.

'Only now I understand why these mini chambers are useful!' said Nitya.

'Useful? For what?'

'There's a young man and woman inside. Go and ask them.'

Amirtham smiled.

When they found themselves alone in another room, Amirtham said, 'I think now we are alone.'

Nitya turned to face him, feigning anger.

She stood before him in her white silk sari dotted with flowers, its red border matching her blouse. Her hands were tightly clasped at her breast, while her look conveyed a pretence at being offended. It fired Amirtham's wistful mind in many colourful ways. He forgot his surroundings. This is the real moment, he thought. Nothing else matters. He eagerly grasped her hands.

'Sahib! Sahib!'

He heard voices from a faraway land – was it history beckoning him? A Muslim caretaker was standing beside him... Had Amirtham turned into Humayun? That would mean... Suddenly Nitya moved away from him.

Good heavens! How could he be so stupid? Didn't he know this was a sacred site?

Amirtham realized he hadn't turned into Humayun and, as per the government rules, he had committed a crime. He had desecrated a hallowed site. The guard might report him to the authorities and Amirtham would face humiliation and a fine.

'Give him something,' said Nitya.

'Will he accept it?'

'Why not? Doesn't he know what's going on in the other room? That wouldn't be happening without his knowledge.'

'You are hundred per cent correct,' Amirtham lauded her. He handed over a five-rupee bill to the caretaker.

'*Aapki bibi hai?*' asked the guard, looking at Nitya.

'*Han ji.*'

The guard's conscience didn't trouble him much – he took the bill.

'Good heavens! You are getting into a romantic mood – of all places – in front of a tomb?' Nitya asked when they emerged from the room.

'The tomb reminds people of their ultimate end. So, the body hurries forward. What's wrong with it?'

At that time, it was a daring act on his part. Now, when Amirtham thought about it, he felt it was very foolish. In a similar situation, today, if he were caught by a guard, could Amirtham defend himself without a sense of shame or indignity?

How does one's age and thinking function? Does one grow wiser with age? Or is it the thinking that makes one act physically old?

He heard the doorbell; he went and opened the door.

'Is Thilakam available?'

It was Mrs Iyer, their neighbour.

For a moment, he felt like saying no, but thought Mrs Iyer's arrival could bring a welcome change in the gloominess hanging about the house.

'Please wait here, I will call her.' He switched on the light in the hall and went to the bedroom.

He tapped on the door.

No response.

'Thilakam, Mrs Iyer is here,' he informed his wife and returned to the hall.

'You have already gone to bed?' Mrs Iyer asked him.

Amirtham didn't answer her question.

'We don't see Mr Iyer nowadays. What happened?' he asked.

'He's too busy with his office work. He's never home before eight.'

The very tone conveyed her pride; she spoke as if the entire central government would freeze but for Mr Iyer's presence.

'Looks like you have returned the Fiat and got a new Ambassador.' What was keeping Thilakam so long? He was forced to chit-chat with Mrs Iyer on trivial matters.

'Yes, the Ambassador is an ideal family car. Now that we are four, the Fiat is too small.'

'Mami, come in,' Thilakam said as came into the hall and joined them.

'You have gone to bed quite early.'

'I was slightly indisposed. What brings you at this hour?' asked Thilakam.

'Am I not welcome, now?' Mrs Iyer asked, smiling.

'I don't mean that. I was just saying this is unusual.'

'Tomorrow they are showing a Tamil movie at Regal. First, my husband said he would go with me, but now he says he can't. I have an extra ticket. I thought you might be interested.'

Thilakam looked at Amirtham; he was quiet.

'Please give her permission – why are you silent?' Mrs Iyer asked him, laughing.

'She doesn't need my permission. It's her decision,' Amirtham said.

'I will come,' Thilakam said.

'Okay. Be at my house at eight,' Mrs Iyer said and rose from her seat.

'Shall I drop her at your place?' asked Amirtham.

'No. I got my driving license. I'll pick her up. Nowadays I do my own driving. You can also teach Thilakam to drive.'

'My husband is too busy to teach me,' Thilakam said.

'My husband was the one who taught me driving!' Mrs Iyer said proudly.

Amirtham didn't fail to notice Mrs Iyer had now raised a new problem for him. Thilakam had been frequently nagging him to teach her driving.

'You can't,' he once told his wife.

'What do you mean?'

'You are not careful. My main concern is that you stay alive.'

Thilakam's naïveté accepted that answer.

But now he was sure Thilakam would never forgive her husband if he didn't teach her after Mrs Iyer got her driving license.

Nitya was an excellent driver. She said her uncle taught her driving. She didn't know what 'slow driving' meant and, even when she drove fast, she had absolute control. Once Amirtham borrowed his friend Nagarajan's car and rode to Aligarh with Nitya. Nitya's mother had to attend to some business at the Aligarh Muslim University. It was Nitya who drove the car.

'Go slow... be careful!' her mother kept warning Nitya throughout the trip.

'It is this very philosophy that ruined our country!' Nitya scoffed and pressed the accelerator even harder.

They arrived at the university.

'I will be done around seven this evening,' Nitya's mother informed her. 'Make sure you return by then.'

After they dropped off her mother, Nitya told Amirtham, 'Let's take a look around the city.' They started on their journey.

'One of my office peons – now old and retired – lives in a village close by; shall we visit him?' Nitya asked Amirtham while driving through the city's streets.

'Sure, why not?'

But they faced a hurdle. They found out that the village was at the back of a large pasture inaccessible to vehicular traffic.

'Must you see him?' Amirtham asked.

'You don't have to come,' Nitya told him. 'You may shop for the Aligarh lock. I will go and see him.'

Amirtham easily sensed the sarcasm in her suggestion that he shop for an item the city was well known for.

'How will you go?' he asked.

A two-wheel carriage drawn by a single horse, its square canopy assembled out of bamboo sticks, came their way. It was like being suddenly thrown back two centuries in time.

'Why not ride this?' Nitya asked. The tanga stopped when she hailed it.

'You really mean it?' The shock in his voice only provoked her laughter.

'You are hopeless,' she mocked him.

'I will go with you.'

The tanga-wala demanded five rupees for the trip there and back. Nitya boarded the carriage, and the ease with which she did so amazed Amirtham. It was not effortless for him.

'Sometimes I am scared when I see how smart you are,' Amirtham confessed to her. Nitya laughed.

Their way to the village – rutted and potholed – seemed impossible even for walking, but the horse made it blithely as if it had mentally grasped all the challenges along its way.

'I don't know how much more I need to sacrifice to prove to you I am not a hopeless person,' Amirtham said.

'I like riding on this tanga,' Nitya said.

Her face indicated she was indeed enjoying the ride. She raised her head slightly and was watching the sky, smiling, her eyes half closed. Amirtham regretted he was not a visual artist.

It was only five in the evening, yet the sky was dyed with a silvery, snowy-white glaze. Amirtham felt his heart swell when some birds in flight appeared like white dots.

'I want to take back what I said earlier about sacrifice,' Amirtham admitted. 'Now I understand what a charming place this is!'

'You always think at your own pace – like a turtle,' Nitya snapped.

Finally, they reached the village – a place hardly touched by twentieth-century civilization. A mud wall surrounding it enclosed some forty families.

Nitya asked about her retired office peon, who went by the name Abdul. As soon as his name was mentioned, a few urchins scurried in four directions to search for him; he was quite well known in that village.

A village elder sporting a large turban invited them to be seated on a charpoy; he was surrounded by five or six old men sharing a hookah with him.

Amirtham and Nitya found themselves the only people dressed in modern clothes. Mr Chowdhary Prasad, the old man, formally addressed them. Then, he had a question.

'*Aap log brahmin hai?*'

'*Kyun?*' asked Amirtham.

'*Han ji,*' Nitya said.

'*Achha ji,*' said Mr Prasad and ordered a boy to fetch drinking water from a Pandit ji's house.

Soon Abdul appeared before them, his face aglow with pride and surprise. He could have never expected that Nitya would think of visiting him. Nitya introduced Amirtham to Abdul and he, in turn, introduced them to the other villagers.

Amirtham realized Abdul knew a bit of English, so he asked him, 'Can't we drink water from your home? Is it compulsory we drink water from the Pandit ji's house?'

Abdul replied in garbled English, 'Ours is an old village that upholds traditional values. Please do not raise new questions and confuse us. We have been living amicably here for the last one hundred years with no Hindu–Muslim problems.'

'How many Muslim families are here?'

'Ten. How does it matter? Come on, let's go around the village.'

The Muslim households were located farther than the rest in the village and, when Amirtham made an observation about it, Abdul offered a reason that baffled Amirtham, 'Most of the Hindus here are vegetarians. How can vegetarians and non-vegetarians coexist in the same locality?'

Was Abdul's opinion based on the lessons he had learned of a viable system? Or, did he firmly believe in separating the two religious groups?

When Amirtham tried to make a point, Nitya intervened, saying, 'Please don't bring in your silly political issues here.' Amirtham loathed her attitude; he was disappointed that Nitya seemed to hold no particular opinions on the prevailing social injustice.

'What would you have done if you were born as a Harijan?' he asked in a blistering tone.

'I know how to deal with that problem when it arises,' Nitya replied.

Amirtham remained quiet during the trip back to Aligarh.

'Dinner is ready. Are you coming?'

Thilakam sounded very friendly. Was it the same person who had yelled at him a short while ago? Mrs Iyer's visit had been a blessing, just as Amirtham had hoped.

He thought of snubbing her, but felt it might lead to a new quarrel. He rose and got ready for dinner.

He noticed it when he settled on the chair: Thilakam's face glistened with a thin veneer of powder, and she had donned a new sari!

The next morning, he remembered as soon as he woke up: Today is the day Thilakam will be going to the movie. He looked at the wall clock. The time was seven. The aroma from the kitchen told him Thilakam was busy cooking.

He welcomed the prospect that Thilakam would be going to the movie. There would be too many complications if Bhanu called Amirtham when Thilakam was at home. He was expecting her call later that morning.

'Haven't you gotten up?'

Thilakam had already showered and was nicely dressed up to go out with Mrs Iyer. Such was her enthusiasm and excitement to see a Tamil movie.

Amirtham arose. For once, Thilakam seemed willing to forgive her husband for all that had happened the previous day.

'Do you want to go?' she asked.

'Go where?'

'To the movie.'

'To the movie? We won't get the tickets.'

'Let's go. No harm in trying.'

'We will not get the tickets,' he repeated.

Why this new harassment? he started wondering.

'Then, I too won't go.'

'Didn't you tell her you will be going?'

'I can just phone her and say I am sick.'

'Then why did you get up this early, dress up and prepare to leave?' He asked while squeezing paste onto his toothbrush.

'You think I should go?'

'You must.'

'Am I a nuisance to you if I stay home?'

Amirtham had the towel draped over his shoulders and was about to start brushing his teeth; he paused and turned to her. *Does she know?*

'What nonsense! What are you saying?' he blustered.

'Why do you keep forcing me to go?'

'Listen to me. You may go or not go, that's up to you. Nowadays, whatever I may say, you seem to think I am hiding something from you.'

Amirtham spoke as if he was justifiably angry at her, but he was frankly scared to imagine she might actually stay home.

'You could have told Mrs Iyer yesterday you didn't want to go. Now, at the last moment, it doesn't sound right to say you are not going. That's all I can say.'

'Well, I am done with all my cooking,' she murmured doubtfully.

'Then you can leave.'

The telephone rang. Thilakam went to pick up the receiver.

Amirtham thought: What if it is Bhanu calling me?

'Hello.' Thilakam was looking at him.

Amirtham wondered: Good heavens! Is that Bhanu? What a disaster! Yet another round of all those episodes of yesterday.

'Mami, I am ready. I am coming.'

I am safe... It's Mrs Iyer on the phone, he sighed in relief.

'Look, I will leave the tiffin, coffee, everything on the table. If you want, you can also have the luncheon items.'

'That's fine. Don't worry. You may leave now – they are waiting for you.'

Before her departure, Thilakam conjured an artificial smile and asked him, 'Have you invited anyone to our house this morning?'

Seething, Amirtham riveted his eyes on her face.

'Please forgive me for asking... I trust you.'

She turned and left. Suddenly, Amirtham felt a tinge of sympathy for her, but she also got on his nerves. Why must I bother about this ritual – an unavoidable tradition in a marriage that restricts my freedom, he pondered. Even as one asserts marriage as a relationship between a husband and wife, doesn't simple logic dictate it should be seen primarily as one between a man and a woman?

Amirtham started on his breakfast. The telephone rang. He stopped eating, walked to the hall, closed the door and picked up the receiver.

'This is Amirtham speaking.'

'Bhanu. Good morning.'

'Good morning. I have been expecting your call.'

'I see. Is Mami home?'

'She's gone to a movie. By the way, don't call her Mami. That tips me off as an old man.'

Bhanu laughed. 'How old are you?'

Amirtham was shocked. Why does she want to know? To deride me?

'Why are you silent? Why not answer me? You are not a woman.'

'Okay... Give me a number below ten.'

'Please! As a child, I never read children's magazines. I don't like them even now.'

Amirtham laughed. 'Let me put it this way: Had I gotten married when I was seventeen, by now I would have had a daughter as old as you.'

'Does this mean you are wallowing in self-pity?'

Amirtham felt as if he had been slapped hard. Here's a smart girl; I need to be careful talking to her, he thought.

'Forget it. Why did you phone me?'

'I kept my promise.'

'What promise?'

'I promised to phone you, and I did.'

'Okay, are you finished?'

'Why are you mad? What are you angry about?'

That was a question he couldn't answer.

'Are you free this evening?' he asked.

'Hmm...'

'Shall we meet in Buddha Park or somewhere else? I need to talk to you.'

Bhanu did not reply at once. Then she broke the silence and asked, 'What do you expect me to say?'

'That I leave to you; I am prepared for any answer.'

Bhanu laughed.

'Why do you laugh?'

'It is funny to listen to you – sometimes you talk like a willing victim.'

Who was talking to him? Was it Bhanu or Nitya? Nitya would have spoken exactly like this, tilting her head slightly to the left, smiling with her eyes to convey genuine happiness...

'I am sorry. I blurted out something I shouldn't have,' Bhanu said.

Amirtham heard her protest and comforted her, 'No, no, this is the way you must talk to me; that's my wish, too.'

'Okay. You may come this evening and pick me up.'

'May I visit your home?'

'Why not?'

The coolness and confidence in her voice was astonishing to him.

'Okay, I will be there at five.'

'Thank you.'

He noticed on returning to the dining table that the dosas had turned soggy and he lost his appetite. He dumped the whole thing in the garbage bin, and washed his hands. When Thilakam returned home, he was fast asleep. He heard the doorbell ring as if in a dream. He woke up and came up to open the door only when Thilakam banged hard on it several times.

On entering the house, Thilakam looked around suspiciously.

'What are you looking for?'

'To see if there's anyone hiding. Why did it take such a long time to open the door?'

'Go ahead – why don't you look under the bed? You are growing crazier day by day.'

Thilakam laid down her handbag on a table and sank down into a sofa.

'Why don't you ask me how the movie was?'

'How was it?'

'First class! A fitting answer to men who are married to a woman and keep chasing other women.'

'How does it end?'

'He ill-treats his wife and indulges in affairs with several women and, finally, he returns to his wife.'

'That's the punishment meted out to him?'

Thilakam cast an angry look at him.

'What are you saying? If you don't like your wife, why did you marry her in the first place?'

'You don't have any sense of humour,' Amirtham told her.

'I don't care if I don't... Come on, let's have lunch.'

After lunch, Amirtham sat on the sofa with a book in his hand. Thilakam sat beside him, her mouth busy with betel leaf and areca nut.

'Just pretend I have gone crazy. Forget this past one week!' she said. She nudged him as she spoke those words, leaving Amirtham wondering: What happened? Did Mrs Iyer offer her a bit of advice?

He sat silent; she leaned her head on his shoulder and asked, 'Why don't we go out?'

'Go where?'

'Buddha Park... Okhla... or some other place...'

He was taken aback. Does she know something? He looked at her searchingly.

'Why are you staring at me? I really mean it.'

Her hand caressed his head.

'We will go another day.'

'Why not today?'

'Today? This evening I am going to Banerjee's. We have a small drinking party.'

Thilakam didn't object to her husband occasionally taking part in a small drinking session; that was one of the privileges she granted him.

'Tell them you won't make it.'

'How can I? This is a party to celebrate his recent promotion. He has also invited a couple of other friends. I can't avoid attending it.'

He was a little amazed that he could so easily and promptly fabricate a lie.

'We will definitely make it next Sunday,' he said.

'Then, I need a favour from you.'

'What is it?'

'Let's now go to the Chanakyapuri–Nehru Park

neighbourhoods. You can teach me driving. Do you know how nicely Mrs Iyer is driving?'

'Listen. I will take you anywhere you want to go; you don't have to bother about driving.'

'Don't sweet-talk me about driving. I am definitely going to drive, and you are going to teach me.'

Amirtham realized any further argument with her would be futile and he rose from the sofa.

'One of these days we must visit that girl, what do you say?' Thilakam remarked.

'Which girl?' Shaken, Amirtham asked as he picked up the book he had dropped on the floor.

'Bhanu. No particular reason. Wasn't her name Bhanu?'

'Why do you want to see her?'

'Didn't she invite us the other day to visit her? Why not go and see her?'

Amirtham knew that Bhanu definitely hadn't invited Thilakam to her home. Yet, he was averse to deny what Thilakam was saying. He remained silent.

'Shall we go? What do you think?'

'You mean barge into her house... just like that?'

'Didn't you go yesterday? Don't get mad at me.'

'I had to drop her off in my car, that's all.'

'I never said you went in on your own.'

'What if I went of my own choice? She's young enough to be our daughter.'

Good heavens! I am turning into a great conman! he thought.

'That's indeed a nice idea! Can I go with you too?'

Amirtham realized he had foolishly fallen into a trap.

'Okay, we will go one of these days.'

'Now I am going to rest. Wake me up when you are ready to leave.' Stretching her legs, Thilakam eased herself onto the bed.

7.

Amirtham held his book in one hand and sat on the bed.

Why does Thilakam want to meet Bhanu? To assess her, judge her as a woman? Bhanu will easily guess what's going on in Thilakam's mind. Thilakam lacks sophistication; she would hardly be able to carry on an intelligent conversation. How could he dodge this situation?

That morning, when Amirtham asked Bhanu if he could visit her home, her prompt response was, 'Why not?' It showed her coolness and confidence. Why? To let him know she was not responsible for any silly fears Amirtham might be entertaining in his mind? Or did Bhanu speak like that just to convey she had neither fear nor respect for her mother?

Yesterday Bhanu had openly admitted to him that she hated her mother. Was it because the mother left the father and moved to the city? Was it possible the mother's actions also played a role in the family drifting apart? Bhanu's mother did look like an opportunist, like she might not hesitate to exploit an opportunity that came along her way.

How different was Bhanu's mother from Nitya's?

Nitya's mother wasn't unaware of Amirtham's friendship with her daughter. She never objected when the two of them visited many places together. Yet, why did Nitya tell him that her mother would never grant her consent for their marriage? Was it a serious mistake that Amirtham committed when he refused to talk to Nitya's mother about her opposition? Instead, he hastily married Thilakam... Maybe Nitya herself decided that Amirtham was not the right man for her; she simply used her mother as an excuse and got out. Now, looking at the woman, fast asleep and dreaming of the movie she had seen earlier that morning, Amirtham felt Nitya was the right woman to be his wife.

Now, recalling his earlier plan to visit Bhanu, he felt a little shadow hover over his mind: phony or real, he had been enjoying peace of mind for twelve years. Should he now cave – just to celebrate his ego? No, he should phone Bhanu and inform her he was not coming... Good heavens, she had no phone!

'What's the time?' Half asleep, Thilakam stirred and asked him.

'Four.'

'Aren't you getting ready?'

'I am getting up.' He got out of the bed.

As Thilakam was coming out of her snooze, Amirtham said, 'You don't have to get up. I can have coffee somewhere outside.'

'How much time do I need to make coffee?' Thilakam said and arose.

Amirtham got dressed and was ready when she served him coffee. She sat down across the table from him.

'Will you be late?'

'I don't know. I will try to make it early.'

'You will be driving. This is a drink party. Don't go overboard.'

Amirtham laughed.

'Did I ever go too far?'

'So far, no.' Thilakam heaved herself up from her chair.

'As a matter of fact, I was thinking if I should go.' Amirtham wiped his mouth with a handkerchief.

'You were saying you made a promise to attend and it wouldn't be nice to break it.'

Amirtham went to the washbasin and gargled. He cleaned his teeth vigorously with his middle finger. Thilakam was staring at him.

'How funny! Why are you washing your mouth after drinking coffee? Where are you going?'

'Why don't you come with me to Banerjee's? Your suspicions will be cleared.'

'Well! As if that's the only thing left for me to do! I just wondered why you wanted to wash your mouth before going out, that's all. Go now and have a good time. Try to come home early if you can.'

Amirtham reached Lakshmibai Nagar, and stopped the car in front of Bhanu's house and honked the horn. Five minutes elapsed; Bhanu didn't show up. Should he turn back? There would be no problem if he simply turned back; he had been given this opportunity to decide his next move.

Should he now return home, he could go out with Thilakam and teach her driving. Thilakam would proudly inform Mrs Iyer, 'My husband too taught me driving.' Finally, when he retired from service and began living on his pension, Thilakam would take over driving when he was tired. That would be a life with no excitement. One of peace... the stillness of a tomb. He honked, again. Maybe Bhanu's mother was sick. He locked the car and got out. The door was shut. Should he go in?

'Hello.'

He turned around. It was Natesan – a man who was involved in every south-Indian cultural association in the city. He served as a secretary in one of them, as a deputy secretary in another, and as a member of the executive committee in yet another one. Whether it was a function to celebrate Vedanta Desikan, the medieval polymath, or Valluvar, the ancient philosopher–poet, he would be a participant, playing a busy and major role.

'What brings you here?' Natesan asked.

'You live around here?'

'Yes. I am in E block. Why don't you visit us?'

'You mean now?'

'Well, if you are visiting somebody, go ahead... Who are you visiting?'

'Is your house close by?'

'If you just turn right, it is the fourth house.'

'Then, come on, let's go to your house.'

'Sure... What about the folks you came to visit?'

'The time is only a quarter after five, and it's so hot,' Amirtham said.

'Yes, it's too hot. Whom are you visiting in this hot weather?'

'I see two or three children in front of that house... Are they yours?'

'Yes.'

'Very active... Are they all your kids?'

'No, no. The one crying is my child. I don't know what my wife is doing inside, leaving him to play in the grass and mud.' Directing the question at himself, he lifted the boy in his arms and entered the house.

'Meenakshi! Meenakshi!'

'Why are you yelling–?'

His wife stopped suddenly when she saw Amirtham.

'Why's the kid crying outside?'

'What else do you expect him to do?'

'This is Mr Amirtham, deputy secretary in the Health Ministry.'

His wife nodded her head as if she had no objection to Amirtham holding that position.

'Please sit down,' Natesan gestured him to a rickety chair. Amirtham wondered why a man actively involved in several social activities never bothered to keep his home spick and span, a little tidier; even a couple of simple cane stools such as modas to seat the guests would have made a difference.

'Get him some coffee,' Natesan told his wife.

'No, please. I don't want any coffee at present. Now, I know where you live; I will visit you another time.'

'How come you want to leave without a cup of coffee in our house?'

'Don't bother now. I will surely visit you another time.'

'I can get you coffee in a minute,' the wife said.

'Look, go and get some coffee. He will have it, only then leave.' Natesan seemed quite determined that he would not let the deputy secretary leave without enjoying a coffee at his home.

And it looked like the coffee had been prepared with the decoction from the previous day. Amirtham drank it despite himself.

Why did I end up like this? he rued. I lied to my wife and wanted to visit someone, but ended up in a stranger's house, drinking horrible coffee prepared by his wife. I am a coward... Surely, I deserve this punishment because I didn't dare knock on Bhanu's door when I visited her.

'I'll see you later.'

Natesan was a little startled when Amirtham suddenly got up to leave.

'You just remembered whom you wanted to see?'

A man prying into others' affairs, Amirtham thought.

'I'll see you some other time,' he said and took off without waiting for any response.

He approached Bhanu's house and pressed the doorbell.

Noticing the window was closed, he examined the front door: it was locked. Was it unlocked when he visited the house earlier? Maybe he hadn't noticed... No, he was sure it was unlocked then. Which meant

Bhanu must have locked it during the time he was visiting the Natesan household. Where could have Bhanu and her mother have possibly gone? Amirtham was confused.

He went back and sat in the car. He began thinking: What should he do? Return home? It made no sense...

Surely Bhanu must have noticed him when he stood in front of her house? Still, she made up her mind to go out. He should have never come.

Should he now visit Mr Banerjee, just as he had claimed to Thilakam? Would he be home? Banerjee was a smart thirty-five-year-old fellow who never married. He had a strong aversion to women. There must be some underlying reason for that.

There was some risk involved in visiting Banerjee. One was likely to end up listening to his boring lectures on Scandinavian folk songs. That would be the punishment meted out to him for wanting to visit Bhanu.

Amirtham steered the car through Sarojini Nagar. Banerjee lived in one of the multi-storeyed government buildings on Ring Road. Amirtham thought, He's a bachelor; why does he need such a big place? That question nagged him every time he visited Banerjee – could it be a sign of jealousy on his part?

Free from social obligations and mores, Banerjee lived in a big home at his own whim and fancy. 'This is a man's world. A woman is an unnecessary infringement to his freedom.' So ran his argument. That didn't mean one could call him an ascetic; he hadn't renounced anything. 'I reserve the right to choose what I want in my life.' That was how Amirtham recalled Banerjee declaring his stand once.

Banerjee was a good painter as well. He never painted anything to win accolades or to display and sell it in exhibitions. When someone applauded his work, he would simply nod his head and talk about something else.

Now, suddenly, Amirtham recalled Bhanu's paintings. One could certainly call them better than average; one of these days he must bring Bhanu to see Banerjee's paintings... I am a damn fool! Then Amirtham thought, again: Why did Bhanu invite me and simply take off?

Now, what if Banerjee was not home? Amirtham

could go and watch some movie in Connaught Place... Today was Sunday, tickets might not be available at any cinema hall... Why not revisit Lakshmibai Nagar? Bhanu could have been visiting someone in her neighbourhood when he showed up at her door. Had he acted impatiently and left in a hurry? Didn't Nitya tell Amirtham once that he was prone to making snap decisions and simply let things roll on? Nitya didn't pay much attention when Amirtham turned angry or lost his poise. There was a time when Nitya wanted to go to Sohna with her office friends and she invited Amirtham to join the group. Amirtham was averse to her going out with office friends.

'Why can't you go another time? We can both go together,' he said.

'Why can't I go now?'

'I am wondering why you want to go with your office friends.'

'You may keep wondering. I want to go with them.'

'You may go, by all means. Enjoy yourself.' Amirtham frowned.

Nitya shrugged her shoulders and laughed.

8.

Nitya and her friends left for Sohna on a Sunday morning. Amirtham, alone at home, was beside himself. He picked up a book to read but could not concentrate. Why don't I go to Sohna? he asked himself. His scooter was out for servicing, so Amirtham decided to go in a taxi. He would be shelling out a lot for the taxi, but Nitya's conscience would surely prick her for rebuffing his advice.

When he reached Sohna, Nitya had just bathed in a sulphur spring, dressed in a new sari and was drying her hair under the hot sun. Her office coworker Mahesh, in a T-shirt, was chatting with her, a cigarette hanging loosely from his lips. Nitya was laughing, both her hands propping her head.

'Amirtham, what brings you here?' Mahesh asked.

Shocked, Nitya turned to face Amirtham.

'Well, you didn't even want to join us–' Nitya began to exclaim when Amirtham interrupted her, 'Am I interfering?'

Nitya sneered, her face reddening.

'Do you want to spy on us? Aren't you shameless? Why didn't you come with us? Why this lone trip?'

Amirtham couldn't help laughing.

'I didn't know you own Sohna to yourself!'

Nitya seemed to calm down.

'How did you come?'

'Took a taxi.'

'Good heavens! That must have cost you a fortune!'

'Don't worry. I felt the urge to see you, so I simply took off. That's all.'

'Why this impulsive behaviour? Some day, this will surely land you in trouble.'

How prophetic she was!

Amirtham reached the multi-storey building where Banerjee lived and stopped. A cricket ball fell at his feet as he locked the car. He picked up the shining ball.

'Uncle ji, the ball...'

A squat, short boy asked for the ball.

'*Tum* bowler *hai yaa* batsman?' Amirtham asked him.

'Fast bowler *hoon*,' said the boy. Amirtham gently touched the boy's cheek and gave him the ball.

Banerjee lived on the fourth floor. A few kids joined Amirtham when he rode the elevator; they were all talking fluently in English about a movie; the topic of discussion was the recent James Bond flick playing at the Odeon.

Banerjee's cook opened the door when Amirtham pressed the doorbell.

'*Aayiye sahib. Babu ji hain.*'

Banerjee was reading a French novel; he was well acquainted with five or six European languages.

'Why are you visiting me now?' was his first question.

'As a matter of fact, I have the same question for you: "How come you are home now?"' asked Amirtham and sat on the sofa.

Banerjee, sitting back comfortably on the sofa, gave no answer. He shrugged his shoulders and stood up.

The room presented an austere look: a wall-to-wall carpet; no works of art except for the one by Banerjee hanging on a wall; an altar lamp suspended from the ceiling – all these seemed to augment the seclusion of the surroundings.

'I sense solitude around here,' confessed Amirtham.

'That's what I prefer as well. I am glad you appreciate that.'

'There's something else I understood today. Deep inside my heart, I think I feel a tinge of jealousy.'

'That doesn't surprise me.'

'I am not saying that to surprise you. I know why I am jealous, but I feel I am stuck.'

Banerjee removed his pipe from his mouth, cleaned it out and filled it with tobacco. He smiled.

'Am I boring you?' asked Amirtham.

'No... go ahead.' He relit the pipe.

'What more can I say?'

'Don't get mixed up in complex issues and theories. Tell me, what's your question?'

Amirtham was silent. Should he open up to him? Banerjee had never been married. How could he possibly understand him? Someone who despised women as poison might actually laugh at what Amirtham told him. On the other hand, who knows, there could be an innate reason for his lifestyle, and he may even reveal it now. What if Amirtham revealed his inner turmoil to him?

What was his question, anyway? Bhanu had snubbed him: after inviting him, she had locked up her house and was gone. Wasn't it then his obligation to simply return home and give Thilakam her driving lesson? A part of his mind refused to acknowledge this commitment; it was caught up rehashing old dreams...

Amirtham noticed Banerjee watching him with a keen eye.

'Are you a computer?' he asked. 'Will you just spit out an answer if I ask you a question?'

'There are no questions – beyond what a man creates on his own,' said Banerjee. He continued, 'In the ongoing battle between Man and Nature, all the problems afflicting a man owe to his visceral nature. The phrase "mental struggle" is what Man has created on his own. I am sceptical about stroking a man's ego.'

'I keep wondering why you haven't spawned a generation of disciples,' Amirtham said, laughing. 'You have all the qualities of a guru.'

'Humour aside, do you agree with me?'

'How can I agree when I can hardly understand you? What do you mean, exactly, by the "battle between Man and Nature"?'

'That battle is called life. The mere fact that a man is alive testifies to his success; death is his failure. So, he carries on with his battle only at a physical level. And he alone – not nature – is responsible for the troubles formed in his imagination.'

'The mere acknowledgement of a man's problems proves their existence. Why do you bring in imagination here?'

'You are a physical entity; why don't you live on mere physical terms? Do you see that dog running after the ball? Does he share any of your concerns? He faces only one problem – how to solve his dilemma *now* – in the *present*.'

Amirtham glanced in the direction Banerjee pointed. Afar, a small white dog with fluffy fur was skipping around a ball, while a few children were clapping their hands, watching the fun.

'I have nothing more to argue with you if that scene doesn't provoke you,' Banerjee continued.

'You are a mere machine. You are totally devoid of human instinct.'

'I believe these are the foolish sentiments that make our lives even more complicated,' Amirtham told him. 'I am not willing to betray my common sense to savour something beautiful that's fleeting and ephemeral. That would mean paying a heavy price. I definitely know what I want in my life. I am trying to get it and will have it.'

The cook served them tea in a teapot, with cups, saucers and spoons on a tray. Banerjee poured himself a little tea.

Amirtham picked up a biscuit from a plate.

Then, the phone rang. Banerjee reached for the phone.

'Banerjee here.'

Then Banerjee looked at Amirtham.

'*Ji haan. Unkey saath baat karnaa hai?*'

He laid down the receiver and told Amirtham, 'Mrs Amirtham.'

Blood rushing through his veins, Amirtham flew into a rage; she was snooping on him. Seething, he picked up the phone.

'What do you want?' The very tone showed his anger.

'Will you be late?'

'Are you into spying? I am still at Banerjee's place. Are you satisfied?' Banerjee, busy lighting his pipe with a match, turned around upon hearing his name.

Why was he getting mad? Was it because Thilakam was checking on him if he was indeed at Banerjee's? Or was he furious because he ended up at the Banerjee house in a state of helplessness?

'Please... don't get mad at me. I know you are not going to lie to me. What I meant was...' She seemed to go on and on.

Amirtham put down the receiver.

'Some kind of trouble?' Banerjee asked.

Amirtham remained silent and stood looking through the window.

Banerjee handed him the teacup. 'Is it hot enough?' he asked.

Amirtham nodded his head in assent.

'Why did you mention my name to your wife?'

'I told her I would be visiting you. She's checking on me.' Amirtham laughed.

'Why's she suspicious?'

Amirtham was silent. He drank his tea and returned the cup to the table. He said, 'You are free to go and do whatever you want to do. Nobody will phone you and check your whereabouts or pry into your activities. You are indeed a lucky man and know how to preserve your freedom.'

'Don't you have within you the power to choose the life you want?'

'Please don't remind me, again and again, how powerless I am,' Amirtham groaned. 'Then, I may start hating you too.'

Banerjee was taken aback. 'What do you mean, saying "you too"?'

'I have begun hating myself.'

'That's a worn-out statement I have been hearing for a long time,' said Banerjee, and laughed. 'You are scared of your own shadow but assume, wrongly, this has to do with your conscience. Who can object if you want to satisfy your ego only by hating yourself?'

'I want to discuss a few things with you. May I?'

'I knew it as soon as you came to see me. Go ahead.'

'May I have a cigarette?'

'I have a pipe.'

'Okay. Let me have it.'

Amirtham lit the pipe, inhaled the smoke a couple of times deep into his lungs, cleared his throat, and began, 'I think I did tell you earlier that I was friendly with a girl before I got married.'

Banerjee nodded his head in agreement.

'A few days ago, I attended a Tamil play. A girl who acted in it reminded me of my old friend; she revived all my deep-seated feelings. It was an invigorating experience for me. I am resentful about the life I am now leading with my wife – it obeys the social mores but is a sham. I revealed my old friendship to my wife and she's outraged: She had been stubbornly clinging to the notion that her husband couldn't be sociable with any other woman. I also happened to meet with that girl, again. I wanted to come to terms with my phony life, so I told my wife about visiting her. Our marriage is now broken but we are kind of patching up and trying to deceive one another as if nothing happened.'

Amirtham broke off when he saw the cook approach them.

'What do you need?' Banerjee asked him.

'Will Babu ji have his dinner here?' the cook asked.

'Yes,' Banerjee answered even as he was attentively watching Amirtham.

Amirtham didn't contradict him.

'Did you tell your wife you will be dining here?'

'Yes.'

Banerjee smiled.

Amirtham continued, 'Just as you have said, I am a weak person; I lack the courage to face reality. I do feel I am now involved in a relationship with the girl who acted in the play. This morning, she phoned me to visit her. We were planning to go to Buddha Park. I went up to her house and waited at her doorstep. Then I happened to meet another old friend. I enjoyed the privilege of spending some time with him – a typical middle-class Tamil family. When I returned from his home, the girl's house was still locked. I decided to visit you because I wanted to shield the lie I told my wife.'

'I still don't understand what your problem is,' Banerjee said.

'As a matter of fact, my intention was to ask you what my problem is.'

'Your problem is you,' Banerjee said, calmly.

'I can see that. Every individual creates his unique personality. Nobody can change it!'

'Please! Stop talking of yourself like you are a Shakespearean character. You loved a girl, gave up on her, married another woman. Now, after twelve years, you seem to have suddenly attained enlightenment under the shadow of a bodhi tree. You are unable to come to a decision, feel quite helpless and are trying to regain peace of mind by mouthing words like personality and fate. I really feel sorry for you.'

'I don't get this: Having invited me to her house, why would she lock it and take off, just like that? She and her mother are the only two people living in that house. Her mother had left her husband a long time ago and moved away. This girl hates her mother; all her sympathies are for her father only; he is now dead. In the beginning, I never understood why she was drawn to me. When I think about it–' Amirtham paused when Banerjee interrupted him, 'You mean, a father figure?'

'You are brutally frank. Yes,' Amirtham answered.

Banerjee smiled.

Amirtham took out a matchstick to relight the pipe. Then he put it down.

'What do you think I should do?'

'Concerning what?'

'What should I do if the situation with this girl grows to be serious?'

'What would you like to do?'

'I want to relive my youth... I would like to experiment – to see if I could bring to life the same emotions, thoughts and enthusiasm of the bygone days. Can I revive my past? Inside every man there's a Yayati lurking.'

Banerjee stood up.

'Okay, shall we eat?'

'Why don't you answer me? Why do you talk about dinner?'

'Whatever you do, be straightforward. I have nothing more to say. I am now hungry, that's the plain truth.'

Banerjee went in.

Amirtham returned home late in the night – on purpose. All of Kidwai Nagar was enveloped in darkness by the time he got there. There was hardly a light in any house in the neighbourhood; on the other hand, lights in several rooms in the medical institute across the street were on. Who knew how many patients were breathing their last at this very moment? Maybe new lives were being born in the nearby Safdarjung Hospital to offset the losses. Yes, nature never rests!

Nearing home, he noticed the light in the veranda was still on, but all the rooms were wrapped in darkness.

Maybe it was a full moon – the moonlight enthralled him.

The man who ironed clothes was asleep at the foot of the staircase. Beside him was his cart.

'*Kaun hai?*'

'*Soya nahi, Sunilal?*' asked Amirtham.

'*Babu ji, namaste.*'

When he pressed the doorbell, he heard the response from Thilakam, '*Kaun hai?*'

'It's me.'

Thilakam opened the door and closed it immediately after Amirtham entered the house.

By the time he went to the room after changing his clothes, Thilakam had already retired to bed.

'What were you thinking? Why did you phone me?' he asked her.

'Just wanted to know if you will be late... you are actually late... Do you know what the time is?'

'Why are you so suspicious about my movements? What would you have done if I was not at Banerjee's?'

'Well, you were there. What would have I done otherwise? Let's talk about it when that situation actually crops up. Now, you may rest... Did you eat lightly at the party?'

'The next time I go out, I need not tell you where I am going. Do you understand? You too are free to go anywhere you want; I too won't question your movements.'

'But... why did that girl phone you?'

Amirtham was stunned. Fortunately, there was no light.

'Which girl?'

'I meant that girl – Bhanu. She asked me if you were available; I said no. She said she was calling for no particular reason. Now, why would she try to call you? How did she get your number?'

'My phone number? I gave it to her. When did she call?'

'Why do you ask? Are you sorry you weren't home when she tried to call you?'

'Nonsense. Maybe her mother was sick, and she wanted to ask for some help.'

'Why should she call you for help? There must be many who would go rushing to help women like her.'

'What do you exactly mean by saying "women like her"?'

'I meant exactly what I said. Now, you may go and rest. We can discuss the rest in the morning.'

Why did Bhanu telephone him? To apologize she was not home when Amirtham showed up? Was her mother sick? When Amirtham first visited Bhanu, her door was unlocked; later, Bhanu locked the door and went out. From where did she make that call? Was it to inform him that they could later meet at some other place? If that were the case, at what time did she actually make that call? Could Amirtham check with

Thilakam? That would set off an earthquake just like last night; Amirtham quietly slumped on the bed.

The next day, on his way to the office, Amirtham decided to visit Bhanu at her workplace at All India Radio. He didn't know in which particular division she worked; he needed to find out. It would be impossible to make that call from his office, so he undertook a personal visit to AIR. Whom should he ask? The receptionist there could certainly help. Many of his friends also worked in AIR and Amirtham was determined he should not be seen by any of them. He recalled Banerjee's counsel, 'Whatever you do, be straightforward.' Could he call his scheme straightforward? Good heavens, why am I so weak? he agonized.

He parked the car in the parking lot attached to AIR and entered the premises when – what a surprise! – he noticed Bhanu afar, walking.

'Bhanu!' he addressed her in a soft voice.

She turned around, startled.

'What a surprise!'

'What happened to you yesterday?'

'Please forgive me... I need to discuss a lot of things with you. When is a good time?'

'To find, once again, your house locked up? I have been already fooled once!'

Bhanu hadn't expected that response – she desperately grasped both his hands, their velvety touch instantly hypnotizing Amirtham.

'If you still trust me, we can meet this evening in any of the Connaught Place restaurants... I need to talk to you.'

Amirtham made no attempt to free his hands from her hold and stood silently for a moment.

'Shall we?' Bhanu asked.

'Okay. Let's go to the Palace Heights. I will see you at six exactly.'

Bhanu's face wore a lingering smile.

'You must not be shocked by my revelations this evening.'

'What revelations?"

'We shall meet this evening... Goodbye.' She left.

What was going to be her appalling disclosure?

That Amirtham refrain from seeing her any longer? Would she insinuate Amirtham in her father's image to involve him in a process of self-revelation? Had Thilakam suggested something to her? Didn't Thilakam say they had not actually spoken anything significant? Could it be something about Bhanu's mother? Had Bhanu fallen in love with some young man? No, she looked like a mature, sensible woman.

9.

Amirtham could hardly concentrate on his work that day. The joint secretary called him to his office to discuss a divorce case. The quality of Amirtham's participation revealed his apathy and indifference.

'Are you sick?' the joint secretary asked him.

'No, I am fine,' Amirtham said.

'If you prefer, we can discuss this another day. We need to make a decision by the weekend,' the joint secretary said.

Amirtham was silent, and made no comment. He knew absolutely nothing about the concerned file; it had been lying unopened on his table for the last three days.

I must peruse its contents today if I am required to discuss the matter with my superior tomorrow, he thought. There was no way Bhanu and that file could coexist in his mind. He went to his cubicle and started going through the file.

He was busy until a quarter to six that evening, discussing the issues and questions raised in that file with the under secretary and section officers. He left his office at six.

Bhanu was standing in front of Palace Heights. She appeared exactly like she had that morning – lively and full of life.

'I was about to go back. I am tired of waiting,' she said.

'Maybe you had to wait fifteen minutes for me,' Amirtham told her. 'I have been waiting twenty-four hours for you.'

'Then I am afraid I owe you another apology,' Bhanu said with a smile, tilting her head to one side. That gorgeous smile refreshed his memory of twelve years ago. It was the same Palace Heights Hotel where Amirtham first met Nitya for a date.

That day, Nitya wore a salwar kameez; she was as stunning a beauty in it as she had looked in a sari. Amirtham stood, his eyes riveted on her.

'Why are you staring at me?' she asked.

'I am not sure I deserve such a privilege.'

'You talk like a hero from our historical novels. You are unqualified for the modern times.'

'What do you mean?'

'These days people don't waste their emotions on words... Anyway, let's go upstairs.'

Nitya moved away to walk to the elevator. Amirtham said, 'Elevator? No.'

'Why?'

'One should never rush and ride the elevator to Paradise; taking the stairs and moving along slowly is more fun... Don't you think so?'

'We won't be staying in Paradise forever... We have to come down...'

'When I said *paradise*, I meant your company...'

Bhanu gently touched his face with the pink kerchief in her hand. The strong scent on it excited him. Bhanu hurried to the elevator.

'No elevator... Let's take the stairs,' Amirtham said.

'Why?'

But he couldn't repeat those words he had spoken twelve years ago; he felt uncertain. Had he already come down from Paradise, just as Nitya had said? Could he possibly soar again?

'Are you saying taking the stairs is good exercise?' Bhanu asked.

'Maybe you are right.'

Amirtham recalled Thilakam frequently reminding him, 'You're past thirty-five. You must go out for regular morning walks. People say physical exercise is good for your health.'

'Stop worrying about me. I am going to live up to eighty years,' he had said.

'You always poke fun at me. Why don't you heed my good advice?' Thilakam had bemoaned.

Climbing three floors proved quite an ordeal – Amirtham struggled for breath.

'We could have taken the elevator. You are gasping.'

How many times had he visited this hotel, climbing the stairs. That was twelve years ago... Scientists have found ways to the Moon – how come they could never bring time to a standstill?

The restaurant was not crowded when they entered. Amirtham was coming after an interval of twelve years and noticed the changes. An old man would be normally seated at the reception counter, now a young man was in charge.

Amirtham asked the young man, 'Any table free?'

The young man pointed towards a table far away in a corner.

'I used to visit this place frequently – that was twelve years ago. Then, an old man was here.'

'Are you talking about Mr Mathur?' the young man asked.

'I don't know his name.'

'He is no more. He passed away two years ago.'

Amirtham was overcome by a strange feeling. Have twelve years wrought a new perspective?

Smiling, he took the table suggested by the young man. The restaurant music was in full swing – some kind of pop tune.

Amirtham noticed most of the patrons were young men and women. There was only one man matching his age – with his wife and family. The wife, her double chin quivering, her voice harsh and severe, was scolding her four or five children for wandering astray. The husband – the head of the family – didn't seem interested in anything. He sat there nibbling on a cigarette, the face indicating he was utterly pleased with everything.

Bhanu swayed her body in step with the music. At first, she sat next to Amirtham; then, she got up and sat down facing him.

'I like this music,' Bhanu said.

'I am pleased that you like it,' Amirtham said.

A young couple was seated a few feet away from their table. The young man, about twenty-two, had long, uncombed curls, sandy coloured, that fell around his neck. His face was milk-white; he wore a T-shirt, buttoned in the back, displaying a rainbow in front. The girl beside him, perhaps twenty, was smiling, putting him under a spell to do her bidding. She was holding his hand and leaning against the sofa while he was whispering something into her ear.

Her eyes were closed, but she was smiling; it was unclear if she was paying any attention to his words.

It was then that the gentleman – the head of the family – arose and left; suddenly, Amirtham felt abandoned.

The music had abruptly grown hysterical.

'My God, what a noise!' Amirtham complained.

'Great music!' Bhanu exclaimed.

This same music – some twelve years ago – hadn't seemed boisterous to him. Presently, youth and exuberance were holding supreme power in this hall; at this instant, Amirtham was hit by a feeling: Did I enter the wrong room? He was scared people were now watching him and enjoying the sight as if he had tripped and fallen down. Twelve years ago, this was the hotel where I lost my youth, he groaned to himself. How can I hunt for it, now?

He thought of suddenly abandoning Bhanu and walking away: she deserved that young man as a romantic partner – the one dreaming of new aspirations and carrying the world on his shoulders – to sit beside her. Why did Bhanu end up in *his* company?

A young man in a black suit, a notebook in hand, approached them. Next to him stood a waiter with a badge, who moved the vase of flowers from the corner of the table to the middle.

'Yes, sar?'

'What will you have?' Amirtham asked Bhanu.

'Hot dog and coffee,' Bhanu ordered. Amirtham too ordered the same, then he told Bhanu, 'I really don't know what you want.'

Bhanu smiled. 'Are you upset even you don't know that?'

Amirtham gazed at her: Nitya too would have said the same thing.

'Why are you staring at me?'

'You said we have a lot of things to talk about... What's going on?'

Bhanu's fingers touched the menu card slightly.

After a while, she asked, 'Do you come to this hotel quite often?'

'This is all what you wanted to talk with me?'

Bhanu laughed, again.

'I felt like asking you, that's all.'

Silence reigned between them for some time. He spoke again.

'As a matter fact, I am coming here after twelve years.'

'I see... Twelve years...', she paused. Amirtham waited for her to finish what was on her mind.

'Twelve years,' she repeated.

He asked her, again, 'Do you see some veiled message here?'

He had been sitting forward, with a hand on the table; suddenly, he sat back.

'Okay, tell me. Why did you want to see me?'

'You were mad yesterday because I called you and then locked my house and left.'

'Will you feel disappointed if I said no?'

Bhanu was half-smiling.

'I know what you mean... But don't think I am fickle minded.'

The server brought the hot dog and a jug of water, and placed them on the table.

Bhanu poured some water in a tumbler and drank it. She wrapped the hot dog in a paper napkin. Then, she began taking small bites.

'Who said you are fickle-minded? Have you begun imagining things on your own?'

'Not really... At my age, anyone would look unpredictable. So, I wanted to warn you not to get the wrong idea about me.'

'You are warning me?'

'Yes. It's a warning. I can't decide easily what I want. But once I make up my mind, I don't suffer any doubt or confusion.'

'Are you done with your talking? Or do you have more to say?'

Bhanu laughed.

'I haven't even started.'

'No! No!' A voice interrupted their conversation. Amirtham turned around. The young lovers at the adjacent table were in the midst of an intense argument. The girl's voice rose higher.

'It's a lovers' quarrel,' Bhanu whispered.

The girl seemed ready to take off when the young man grasped her hand impetuously and tried to make her sit down. Protesting and jerking her hand free, the girl pulled away from him and made a dash for the exit. The young man threw a ten-rupee note on the table – he didn't even bother to see the bill – and ran after her.

'He must be her pet,' Amirtham said. 'He keeps wagging his tail.'

'Why single him out? Nowadays all young men act like pets. They are only good enough to catch and return a ball thrown at them. If some American boys sport hairdos, they too shamelessly ape their style. What a horror!'

Why does Bhanu hate young men? Her voice indicates she turns emotional when she utters these words; Nitya would have never spoken like this; Bhanu is older and wiser – was she speaking from her own experience? Or is there some other reason for her aversion to young men? She's saying she needed to talk about a lot of things; is this a tip off?

Bhanu finished eating her hot dog and wiped her hand on a paper napkin.

A waiter now served them coffee. Bhanu used the sugar tongs to pick up a sugar cube from the tray and asked him, 'How many?'

'Two.'

She gave him two cubes in his coffee and dropped one into her own cup.

'Are you avoiding the second cube because you think you may put on weight?'

'No. I hate sweets.'

'I can see that... Youth is sweet, but you seem to hate it.'

'When you think of the human life cycle, the transition from infancy to boyhood, boyhood to youth and youth to middle age – all those moves ought to take place gracefully. We saw just now how that young man was grovelling before the girl. You still believe youth is sweet?'

'I think there must be a strong reason why you talk like this.'

'I have been telling you all this time. You are not convinced?'

'No, I am not convinced!'

She drank her coffee in one gulp.

'What more do you want me to say?'

'I am willing to hear anything you want to tell me.'

'You better get a tape recorder,' Bhanu said, and laughed. 'You may find it useful.'

'What more can I say? You were saying you have a lot of things to talk about; that's why I am here. But we seem to be still talking in circles.'

'You are right. That's what we are actually doing. What's the reason?'

'Shall I tell you?'

'Say it. Why do you talk like you are threatening me?'

'These are my hunches – they could be right or wrong. First, yesterday, up until the evening, you hadn't made the decision to see me, so you might have gone out somewhere. Second, your mother might resent my visiting you at home, so you wanted to avoid the embarrassment of welcoming me, so you left home, but tried to make a phone call from another location. Third, you still haven't figured out a reason, can't make up your mind, so you keep stringing me along.'

Bhanu tipped her head back slightly, and laughed.

'Everything you said is wrong.'

'I didn't say they couldn't be wrong.'

She summoned one of the waiters passing by and told him, '*Aur do* cup coffee *laana*.' Amirtham stared at her in utter surprise.

'Only now are we about to begin our conversation,' she asked.

Amirtham prepared himself to listen to her; folding his hands together, he leaned against the sofa. Bhanu cleared her throat and began, 'Yesterday, I didn't go out anywhere. I saw you coming and waiting for some time on the veranda. Earlier, Mother and I had a big argument; she insisted I must not see you, talk to you or go out with you; she locked me inside the house and left. When she returned, I went to another house and made the phone call to you.'

Amirtham remained silent for a while. Then he asked her, 'Why do you think your mother hates me?'

'Which mother do you think would approve of her unmarried daughter hanging out with a married man?'

Amirtham found himself hard-pressed to answer her question.

10.

Why would Bhanu tell me this? Amirtham was thrown into speculation. Was she referring to a predisposition of the public at large for scandal while also implying that her mother was misinterpreting their relationship? Was this some kind of warning she was hurling at him? Given that Amirtham was already married, was she discreetly raising the question, 'What are you going to do about it?'

'Why do you have to argue with your mother if you understand what she's saying?'

'Just as I told you before, I can't easily make up my mind; once I make a decision, I don't waver. Now that I've decided to socialize with you, I am not going to mind what she says. This ended up as a row because, like my mother, I am also a strong person. She locked me up and left. But, later, I made the phone call I wanted.'

'Why were you so keen to see me?' Amirtham wanted to know.

'I never thought you so naïve that you don't know the answer to that question.'

Her remarks triggered a thrill as well as panic in him: the chess board had been set up. He must play and move his pieces.

'Can I ask you a question?'

'That's what one calls the "Victorian approach".'

'Whatever it is... Do you know my age?'

'Don't ask me such foolish questions. It might go against my present opinion about you and cause disappointment.'

'How can you call it foolish? You are at an age prone to emotions; I meant to say I am well ahead of them.'

'So, it was your sense of detachment that brought you to my office this morning? Mr Amirtham, you make me laugh!'

Amirtham gulped his coffee. He was a little afraid to look at Bhanu.

'I don't understand why you don't like young men.'

'Just as you were saying, there could be some powerful reason,' Bhanu said, and laughed.

'Here's my gut feeling... A few more ideas–' Amirtham began.

'As usual, they will all be wrong. Your first hunch might be that some young man entranced me and then deceived me. If so, that's wrong.'

'Okay. I won't make any guesses. You can tell me.'

'Remember the young fellow who ran after that girl? Someone similar to him, who had just begun sporting a scanty moustache, was once friendly with Mother in Madras... One day, that idiot's parents visited our home. My God, the outcry they caused! They took it for granted that Mother was not really interested in their son but had actually "procured" him for me! I was not willing to give them any further shocks.'

Bhanu mentioned this without feeling any embarrassment and discomfiture.

'Are you surprised that I am stating all this rather blithely? Listen, I have been emotionally revisiting this horror so often, it has lost all its shock value.'

Even as she spoke, she grasped the glass tumbler on the table and glared at it. Was it the fury directed at her mother or the disgust provoked by those young men? Why did she keep tightening her grip, as if to crush the tumbler?

'I don't want to live with Mother. I need to get away from her.'

Did it mean Amirtham would be a catalyst for that separation?

'You believe I could – I can – give you the security?'

'Nonsense – I don't care about security. I like you. I can't explain why. We both share common interests; that could be a reason.'

'I am now looking at the first woman who doesn't care for security. The very reason women get married has to do with the feeling of security.'

'It is not surprising that in a society where men play a central role, the women seek security. For the Indian woman, the husband confers the main status; it's enough even if he simply exists, or is only alive. Our notions of marital fidelity being what they are, what more can you expect?'

'Does it mean you want to carve out a life of your

own – distinct from the rest? That's why you expect my friendship?'

Bhanu gave no immediate reply. She kept on staring at him.

'Why are you staring at me?'

The smile on her face suggested a trace of sarcasm.

'What makes you think everything in life should have a reason? You don't trust yourself?'

Amirtham was dumbfounded; Nitya had asked him the same question several years ago. And she was quite open and direct about it – 'Are you lacking self-esteem?' was her question; now Bhanu was displaying tact and subtlety. Amirtham never doubted he suffered from self-doubt and apprehension. Because he never matched Nitya's zest and passion for life, he excused his receding into obscurity. But now? Could he claim his age as a pretext? It is said, in foreign countries, that a man's life starts at forty. But in our country? No, forget it! Age is the only reason why one dwells on these useless thoughts.

'Please excuse me if I offended you,' Bhanu said.

'No, no... You asked me, "You don't trust yourself?" I was mulling over it.'

'What do you mean by "mulling over"? Do you have a lot of things on your mind?'

'I have asked a lot of things about you. But you don't know anything about me. Am I right?'

Bhanu shrugged her shoulders, as if she didn't care.

'I won't say it if you are not interested,' he said.

'Why do you avoid talking about the present? I hate to dwell on the past.'

'I think you have stubborn confidence in yourself.'

Bhanu smiled; she seemed to agree with him.

Then, a young man arrived on the scene. He was six feet tall, his face showing detachment and youthful vigour. He displayed no interest in examining his surroundings; he was carrying some English magazines; he sat on a nearby sofa and began turning over the pages.

Bhanu turned towards him; she continued to look at him for several seconds – it was certainly a face well deserving of such attention. Amirtham felt his hair had grown a little greyer.

Aware that Amirtham was noticing her, Bhanu cast her glance on the magazines in the young man's hand, and said, 'Looks like he has chosen the right place to read.'

'I feel a little awkward that he's alone – all by himself,' Amirtham said.

'Shall I give him some company?' Bhanu asked, laughing.

'Go ahead... That might be the most fitting thing to do.'

Bhanu tilted her head slightly. Then she suddenly caught both of Amirtham's hands, held them in hers, and said, 'I think getting older has become your obsession!'

Amirtham felt as if he had been slapped hard; he turned aside to gawk at a blank wall. Thanks to Bhanu's words, the pleasant sensation from her touch smashed to smithereens, and he fretted.

It was true; his obsession became a barrier while his conscience played all kind of games, weakening him further. The young men in his vicinity bolstered that feeling. Just as Bhanu said, Amirtham's predilection to compare himself with others must stem from his lack of self-confidence.

He pressed down slightly on her hands holding his. Taken by surprise, Bhanu turned her gaze towards him. Now, she looked even more alluring. Why should I think I am getting older? Amirtham wondered. Now, he could see the revelation in Bhanu's eyes was gone and her face had reddened. Amirtham grasped her hand with his fingers.

'Just as I was saying, you have mustered all your anger to prove to me you suffer no obsession,' she said with a laugh.

Amirtham freed his hands.

'Shall we go?'

'The bill?'

Amirtham called the waiter and paid the bill. They silently walked out.

'The time is eight,' Bhanu said when they reached the street.

'It has gotten too late to go home...' Amirtham said.

Bhanu made no reply.

She remained quiet until the car reached Lakshmibai Nagar.

When they reached her home, Bhanu said, 'I am very happy today – after several days... Do you know why?'

'I suppose you never make decisions quickly. Today you seem to have made a quick one!'

'Yes, that's also a warning to you.'

'A warning?'

'Yes, you are the one who persuaded me to make this decision. So, your responsibility also gets a boost.'

Amirtham was a little frightened by the composure in her tone and her steely resolve.

'Okay, when can I see you again?' She pulled his hand from the steering wheel and shook it. Amirtham was quiet.

'How about tomorrow?' She got out of the car.

'Tomorrow?'

'Why, are you hesitant?'

'Okay... Where do we meet?'

'Let's go to a different place. How about India Gate?'

'Not tomorrow. Why not next Sunday?'

For a moment, Bhanu fixed her eyes on him.

'Are you scared of me?'

'What do you mean? Why should I be scared of you? I am not an interesting enough person for overly frequent encounters.'

Bhanu smiled.

'I think with a few more outings, you will gain self-confidence. Let's meet tomorrow. Please visit me at five in the evening. Ta-ta... Bye-bye.' She was gone.

When Amirtham reached home, the front door was unlocked. This was something he had not anticipated. Thilakam was in the hall, reading a book. Amirtham was a little doubtful if it actually was Thilakam; he verified it two or three times. That's how she was dressed: a sari tightly wrapped around the body; the hair fashionably coiled to match the well-groomed face; her choice of the sari as well as the manner in which it was draped around her body made her a little slimmer than usual. Amirtham felt someone must have advised her in the choice of clothes and make-up.

Thilakam rose when she saw him.

'Why are you this late?'

'Forget my being late... Why this lavish display today?'

'No particular reason. Do you think I should look gloomy and cheerless when you return home?'

'Like this...' Amirtham began, but didn't finish what was on his mind, and sat down on the sofa.

'What are you trying to say?'

'Who taught you this make-up?'

'What makes you ask me such a question? You think I am just an illiterate village girl?'

'No, no... What I meant was, until now you have never tried this kind of make-up.'

'Well, until now you too didn't hang around with some strange woman! You have only just begun.'

Amirtham, who was busy untying his shoes, stared at her.

'What did you say?'

'I am not ignorant of any of your activities, you better keep that in mind! Tell me, I have a question for you. Why did you become so deranged?'

How in the world did she find out? Who could have spilled the beans? Amirtham was sure none of his acquaintances was aware of his trysts. Even if someone was, would they care to inform Thilakam?

Thilakam now approached and sat next to him.

'Tell me what's wrong with me. Am I dark in complexion? Are you bothered because I am not a good talker like you? What can I do about it? I can only be myself.'

Amirtham rose from the sofa. He recalled the novel *1984*: its refrain, 'Big Brother is watching you' had now become a reality. He never imagined Thilakam could deploy spies all over Delhi to poke around in his private movements; he was certain Thilakam was incapable of such an operation.

He went to his room and changed. He thought, why would Thilakam see their predicament as a battle for self-protection – rescuing their shaky marriage? She couldn't possibly see it as anything else. This evening, all of Amirtham's pent-up emotions had found an outlet; Bhanu too had made no attempt to hide her feelings. What were Amirtham's future plans? He needed to discuss them with Bhanu.

Did it make sense to mess up his current serene life? It could be the stillness of a tombstone or something else. Did he have the courage to create new circumstances and face them head on? Back then, Nitya called Amirtham a coward – not directly – but in so many words. Today, Bhanu scoffed at him for lacking self-confidence. Just as Hamlet said, did conscience make Amirtham a coward?

When Amirtham returned from his room, he noticed Thilakam standing near the dining table, ready to serve him food.

'I won't eat. I am not hungry.'

She turned round.

'Why?' She asked the question in a hard voice.

He gave no answer, and sat down on the sofa.

'Who told you?'

'What? Told me what?'

'I mean... what happened this evening.'

'Why do you care who told me? Is that important?'

'When someone twists facts and spreads rumours about an innocent conversation, don't you think it is important to know who started the gossip?' asked Amirtham.

'If the conversation between you two is routine, why would the girl's mother phone me and reveal everything?' Thilakam asked.

Amirtham understood now. What Bhanu had said about her mother was all true. It was now confirmed that the mother was dead against her daughter's behaviour. How should a mother react to her daughter hanging around with a married man? Not just a married man, but a much older one. My God, how could I lose my head! Amirtham rued.

Thilakam came and sat beside him.

'Hereafter, I will act as you wish... Just stop doing the naughty things that the girl's mother told me about.'

'Naughty?'

'Yes. What else would you call that kind of wayward behaviour? Had we been blessed with a daughter, by now, she would be seventeen or eighteen...'

'That's not true. Why are you so desperately fond of pointing out that I am old?'

'Are you doing all these things to prove you are still young?'

Amirtham was taken aback. Could this be true? He had never expected Thilakam could so easily assess the situation.

Should he admit his youthful days were behind him? Bhanu's involvement with him was also based on the same criterion. She had addressed him as 'Mama' on her first encounter with him; she also gave the reason why she was with him – because she disliked young men. Was Amirtham really in love with Bhanu? Or was it sympathy towards someone who served as a catalyst to revive his youthful dreams?

Overcome by myriad feelings, he closed his eyes; the most sensible thing would be to live in the present, dictated by the calendar.

He never had the guts to take up any of life's

challenges. On the other hand, the one now seated across him – his wife – was stubbornly clinging to the present. This was the truth, and if Amirtham took a stand, he would find himself set free from stress and strife.

He went and lay on the bed. Soon, he clearly heard Thilakam heaving a deep sigh; she kept on talking to him, but his ears never heard the words. At this time, he needed her, only her: Thilakam. The next day, he woke up very late. A multitude of disparate thoughts and dreams had occupied his mind all night.

Suddenly he had a sensation that he and Thilakam had grown old; one couldn't actually call it a dream because they both were still aware and alert. Had Thilakam's hair turned completely grey? Amirtham touched it. Thilakam opened her eyes.

'What do you need?'

'Nothing.'

'Whom were you imagining?'

He went back to sleep. On the bedroom walls he could see the shadow play of the trees just outside the window; there were several spellbinding images between dream and wakefulness – such as Nitya's face, Bhanu's smile – interposing themselves in the dreams.

That majestic young man he had seen at the hotel appeared in his dream as a gigantic figure reaching up into the sky, hovering from the clouds and peeping at the ground below. Alone, Amirtham was left high and dry, beseeching liberation, in a vast expanse where the eyes could see nothing but sand stretching for miles and miles. He heard an echo that chased him like a shadow and petrified him.

He struggled hard to bring some logic and order to his dreams, to no avail.

'Are you not going to office today?'

He turned around. It was Thilakam, after a shower, clad in a new sari, with a bunch of flowers adorning her hair.

He got off the bed.

'Why don't we go out somewhere if you are not going to work?'

'Go where?'

'Nehru Park. You can teach me driving.'

Silently, Amirtham walked to the bathroom.

'This is what I hate... Why don't you answer me?' he heard Thilakam whining. He welcomed the idea of not going to work; that was how he would avoid seeing Bhanu. Well, why was he scared of her? No, he was not scared, but must he see her every day? But today he couldn't avoid teaching Thilakam to drive.

After returning from the bathroom, he prepared to read the newspaper.

'Do you know the time?' Thilakam asked.

'Tell me.'

'It's eight. Have you decided not to go to office?'

'I did...but you are forcing me to give you driving lessons.'

Thilakam laughed.

'Stop worrying. No driving lessons today. We will just take a ride into the city.'

'Where do you want to go?'

'How about Karol Bagh? I need to do some shopping in Ajmal Khan Road.'

He didn't ask Thilakam about her shopping needs; he never did.

He was drawn to some items in the newspaper and was intently reading them.

'Why are you silent? Shall we go?'

He didn't respond.

'I keep asking and you are silent... You don't want to go out with me?'

'Where?'

'Where? This is how you feel whenever you want to take me out... Am I not fashionable enough to go out with you to a hotel?'

Amirtham folded the newspaper. She was getting on his nerves. He rose, silently, from the chair. The best punishment he could mete out to Thilakam was to let her know he was not affected by her words. He also felt she was not sophisticated enough to know it. So, he said, 'Okay, now I am going to the office.'

'You are going to the office?'

'Yes.'

Thilakam could no longer contain her mounting anger.

'You don't mind going to a hotel with a stranger – a woman – but you don't want to come with me for shopping?'

'Yes, that's my choice.'

'What did you say? Your choice? *Your choice*?'

Incensed, Thilakam rushed and dashed her head against a wall. Amirtham galloped behind her to pull her back.

'Whatever happened to you? Are you suffering from hysteria?'

'Yes! This is hysteria! I am crazy! I am a fool! I have failed to hold on to your love for me! I am lost!'

Dragging her to a sofa, Amirtham forced her to sit; Thilakam covered her face with both hands and began to sob.

'Listen, why are you upset? What happened? Am I dead?'

She got up and left the room. Amirtham was disappointed because he had expected another sentimental response from her. He thought she might feel some relief after venting her anger in an emotional outburst. But Thilakam seemed to have felt enough emotional fulfilment after the encounter. Did she feel like taking a break? She disappeared into another room and shut the door behind her with a bang. The blast hit Amirtham like a slap.

That evening, after work, Amirtham visited Akashvani Bhavan, the AIR building, where Bhanu was waiting for him. She hopped into the car and sat next to him.

'What happened in your home yesterday?' she asked.

Astonished, Amirtham gaped at her.

'I know everything. Mother said she told your wife everything. She's determined that she should stop me from seeing you. But I certainly know she can't do anything about it.' How could Bhanu talk about this with a smile? While Amirtham was still fretting over his clash with Thilakam that morning, she didn't seem a bit concerned about her mother's opposition. Maybe her formative years could offer some explanation for her behaviour. On the other hand, she might be seeking Amirtham's company to openly demonstrate her hostility to her mother. And she seemed to be really relishing this entanglement! But could Amirtham endure this quandary – a situation pitching him in a conflict with his wife?

Ugh! One must stop thinking. Just move with the flow, looking at events as they come and go, with no concern for pros and cons... That's how you justify your actions... What if the woman next to you is Bhanu or someone else? She represents a moment – an event in your life... The past too was once a parade of events and happy moments... Every event ends within an allotted time... We are either wide awake or fast asleep, experiencing or remaining inert, acting or staying passive, acting or daydreaming... Everything in nature is destined to end. Doesn't science validate this? The physical world doesn't concede continuity, does it?

'Now, where are we supposed to go?' Bhanu asked. Amirtham felt her voice coming from a distant land. Given the state of his mind, he felt he was obliged to answer her.

'How about spending some time in a hotel?'

Taken aback, she turned to him. She gave no reply.

'Shall we?'

She nodded her head.

That hotel must have been a Mughal-era landmark in Old Delhi. The rooms were small, each with a wall at one end and a wooden partition at the other. The colour of the bedspread had begun to fade, but the satin cloth had a weird glossy look.

Freed from the surrounding proscriptions and probing eyes, seeking unlimited abandon in the secluded room, primed for a tryst, Amirtham and Bhanu exchanged glances.

'We seem to have gone back a hundred years,' Bhanu said.

'This is the time to realize our unfettered freedom,' Amirtham said.

Bhanu, who sat on a nearby chair, laughed.

'Why do you laugh?'

'You have travelled to Old Delhi and sneaked into this ancient Shah Jahan Hotel, yet you talk of freedom. What are you scared of? Why do you need this hideaway?'

Amirtham hadn't expected this. What was he scared of? Just as Bhanu said, did 'unfettered freedom' mean the courage to closet yourself in a faraway place with a totally non-existent opposition? If so, why did Bhanu acquiesce to accompanying him to this hotel? Was it her enthusiasm for a new experience? Or did she want to test how valiant Amirtham was in facing life's challenges?

'Are you angry?' she asked.

'Hmm...' Amirtham let out a deep sigh. Then he remembered and hastened to add, 'No, no.'

Bhanu rose from the chair to rest on the bed. Before doing so, she picked up the bedspread. Instantly, she smelled the disgusting odour from under the stinking cot.

'What a horror!' She recoiled in revulsion.

'I am sorry. Let's go to another hotel,' Amirtham said.

Bhanu raised a corner of the cot and dropped it back down. Its woven material – cotton rope – smelled worse than the bedspread.

She sat on the edge of the cot.

'Have you been here before?' she asked him.

'What makes you ask me that?'

'Have you been here before?'

Amirtham gave no reply. Yesterday, when he tried to tell her his past life, she was not ready. But, now, she raised that question with a touch of aloofness. She seemed totally unconcerned about any reply he might proffer.

'Bhanu, I want to ask you a few questions.'

Bhanu was a little surprised.

'What's this? You need my permission to ask any questions?'

He sat down on a chair. It leaned to one side, but he steadied himself.

'So, you are willing to listen to me?'

'Depends on what you are going to say.'

'Before I married Thilakam, I was friendly with another girl. Her name was Nitya.'

'Is that important?'

'What?'

'Her name.'

Amirtham was stunned. Then he said to himself: Yes, it is true. Why should I mention her name?

'Okay, forget her name. She resembled you – in manner, speech, everything.'

Bhanu laughed. Amirtham was discussing a serious matter and he didn't appreciate her laughing.

'Are you mocking me?'

'No, no, I thought you might be chasing her image. That made me laugh.'

'I couldn't marry her.'

'After marriage, where is the need for an image? Maybe you are happy chasing the image.'

'You may be right. I don't know what would have happened if I had married her.'

'You would have found out that the Nitya you had thought was Nitya was not the one you got married to. You would have discovered a lot of difference between the "friendly" Nitya you had socialized with and the Nitya you had married.'

'You are very cruel,' Amirtham told Bhanu.

'Where's the cruelty here?' asked Bhanu. 'The human tendency is always to idolize those we admire for some reason or the other. But it doesn't necessarily mean they will turn out to be like the person of our imagination.'

'Are you talking about me, or about yourself?'

Bhanu smiled. 'Mr Amirtham, you are very smart.'

'What do you think of me?'

'I didn't expect you would bring me to this hotel. I can understand what happened last evening; but why are you scared of your own shadow?'

'I offended you by bringing you to this hotel...'

'All right – are you ready to divorce your wife and marry me?'

'*What?*' Amirtham's voice rose to a shout, unable to contain his shock.

Bhanu was laughing; it took her a minute to stop.

'That girl - what's her name - Nitya? I can see why you couldn't marry her. I can now understand your *courage* when you brought me to this hotel... Mr Amirtham, you have lost all my respect for you.'

Amirtham felt as if whiplashed. Just as she had shoved aside the dirty bed, Bhanu now cast off his attraction like a bundle of dirty clothes.

Divorcing Thilakam was just impossible - it was something Amirtham could not even think of. Thilakam would never consent to divorce on any grounds. How can a mere law reform the prevailing social order of a society founded with the husband playing a principal role? Thilakam might not be wholeheartedly devoted to her husband. But, in our society, more importance is accorded to the husband's title than to the husband himself. Didn't Bhanu say it yesterday? Not only that; a woman is entitled to the honour of being called a sumangali when her husband is alive; this custom confers a unique privilege on the husband. Did Amirtham have enough courage to go against society?

'Shall we go?' asked Bhanu and got up.

'We can leave if you want. But you need to listen

to what I have got to say. We are now living in a dysfunctional world. Some fifty years ago, in the twenties, my grandfather had three wives; nobody raised their eyebrows. Now we live in a society that asserts equality between sexes; we hear people talking about moral order: "One woman for one man!" Our laws talk about divorce, but how many people think of it as an option? We are trapped: We are scared to use the new laws while decrying our tradition and custom as uncivilized!'

'Okay, let's go.'

Annoyed, Amirtham stared at her. With her arms folded, Bhanu looked away.

Amirtham locked the room and they left.

They were silent till the car crossed Ajmeri Gate and approached Hardinge Bridge. It was Bhanu who broke the silence when they reached Connaught Place.

'Until now I hated boys. Only now I understand. As far as men are concerned, there's no difference between boys and men. All are idiots. Am I right?'

Amirtham gave no reply.

'My idealistic instinct makes me sympathize with your incompatible marriage,' Bhanu began. 'However, when it comes to men like you – they lack courage, and act like the heroes in our tragic plays. They are all half-baked idealists who want to soar high. Their only problem is they have no wings and never get off the ground. They can never solve their personal problems. You are all opportunists.'

'I have heard of a particular group of women in a foreign country – they hate all men.'

'What do you mean?'

'You too may end up like that.'

'Is that a curse or a compliment?'

Amirtham was silent and drove on. Does every woman harbour hatred for some man? Similarly, does every man secretly nourish revulsion for some woman? Didn't psychologists describe Don Juan, the lover and seducer of women, as a woman-hater? Could sexual attraction serve as a means for both men and women to avenge themselves on one another?

Maybe he should not have confided to Bhanu about Nitya. Bhanu didn't directly admit she was hurt by Amirtham's revelation – she was smart, and invented some other pretext to end her relationship with him. Which woman with a modicum of self-respect would welcome a man's declaration, 'I am interested in you because you remind me of my former girlfriend.'

The car stopped near Safdarjung airport. Rehearsals were in progress for the upcoming Republic Day celebrations. The road barrier was down because the helicopters, hovering up in the darkening sky, were about to land.

'The helicopter is coming down!' Amirtham said. Bhanu smiled.

'When I first met you, I thought you were a simple girl.'

Bhanu smiled, again.

'Can I say something else?'

'Sure – go ahead.'

'Were you jealous because I mentioned Nitya?'

Bhanu reacted with loud laughter.

The gate was now open. Amirtham started the car. Why does Bhanu laugh?

'I have no objection if you feel happy imagining all these things,' Bhanu said. 'You may continue to do so.'

He steered the car towards Lakshmibai Nagar.

'This is the last time I am visiting the area. I won't be coming here any more,' Amirtham said.

'If someone turns out so sentimental, there must be something fundamentally wrong with him,' Bhanu said.

'Okay, you have arrived.'

After Bhanu got down, Amirtham didn't wait to bid Bhanu goodbye; he turned the car in the direction of INA Colony.

On reaching the house, he found it was locked.

Could Thilakam have gone to the market? Usually, around this time, she would not. The locked door swelled the emptiness in his heart. He stood there for a long time. Should he go away?

Where could he go? Nobody needed him.

The world teases him, provoking him again and again – everyone stands aside, enjoys his scuffle, and boos.

Should he go in? He always has a spare key. What if his loneliness heightens at home, and torments him?

The new issue of *The Hindu* lay on the doorstep, It was normally delivered at five in the evening; so

Thilakam must have left home well before five. Where could she have possibly gone?

He went in – the whole house was enveloped in darkness. He noticed a letter on the table. He hurried and opened it.

'I know about your whereabouts. Where's the need to prolong our family farce? I can take care of myself. Thilakam.'

He felt his body trembling as he finished reading it. He crushed the paper and put it in his shirt pocket.

Bhanu's mother must have spied on him and informed Thilakam. He seethed with anger. Where could Thilakam go? She had no close friends. Except for her immediate neighbourhood, she never ventured out alone.

He phoned Mrs Iyer in the next block.

Mr Iyer answered the phone.

'Yes, Iyer here.'

'This is Amirtham speaking. Is my wife there?'

'Your wife? I don't think so. Let me check...' Amirtham heard him call out to his wife. He spoke again into the phone and confirmed that Thilakam had not been to their house.

Further telephone calls to five or six locations didn't help, either. Everybody wanted to know what had happened to Thilakam, causing him more aggravation.

Could she actually be at home and just testing him? Amirtham went searching every room. Then he rebuked himself, Why am I acting stupid? She has actually locked the house and gone out! Then, why look for her in the house?

Amirtham found his dinner had been prepared and served on a plate, covered and set upon the dining table. Thilakam had completed all her chores before leaving the house.

What should he do now? Report to the police? 'My wife is missing! Please find her!' What a shame. Maybe he should wait till the next morning... *What if she acts desperate and does something?* No, she was not that kind of woman.

He shut the front door and slumped on the bed. He had been thinking of forgetting the twelve years of his life. Now, it had become a reality. Tonight, his company would be his loneliness and his dreams.

Now, human life exists in two orbits: The first, the interior one, is when the whole world becomes a man's home; he learns the life's lessons and accepts his obligations. In the other, the exterior one, he recognizes the limits to his personal freedom. Presently, does that latter freedom make Amirtham happy?

The silence in the house colluding with the stillness of the night terrorized him. The unoccupied bed beckoned, 'Are you enjoying your new freedom?'

'Are you coming to dinner?' He heard a soft voice inviting him from near the dinner table, but he saw only vessels stacked in a row – nothing else.

He went out to the balcony. Across the street, a series of hospital buildings came into his view, all of them dazzlingly lit against the night sky. In that vast glimmering world, he was just a dot – but endowed with thinking and personal freedom!

The unruly goat that drifted away from the flock and the mouse caught in a trap are scared of freedom. Society was an inevitable trap. Man should be either totally virtuous or totally stupid – only then does he realize his credo of personal freedom.

That trap alone is heavenly. Amirtham returned to the bed. Prudence dictates that one tries to bring a sense of clarity and order to this messy and complicated world. That's the test of character life demands of every man. Amirtham could no longer act desperate and hope to soar high with a broken wing. His infatuation with Bhanu was appealing yet fleeting – like a lovely plume of nascent cloud floating in the air – and it only added to his misfortune.

Let the world be a trap, he can't live by himself. He must find Thilakam... It is only in his loneliness that he recognized his problem was him. Thilakam alone could save him...

Where is Thilakam?

Then the telephone rang.

Translator's Acknowledgements

I appreciate Mr Indira Parthasarathy's support and confidence in me when he granted me the permission to translate his novel.

I am grateful to my daughter Anu Sukhdial who extensively reviewed the early draft of the manuscript. She provided valuable assistance in revising and reworking the text in light of our various exchanges with the Hachette India editing team.